STEPHANIE COLSON

Savage Protector

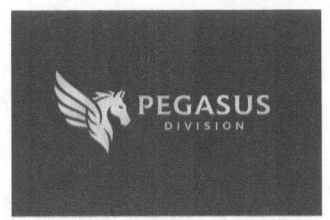

First published by Mark Wisnewski 2025

This novel is entirely a work of fiction. The names, characters, and incidents portrayed in it are the work of the author's imagination. Any resemblance to actual persons, living or dead, events, or localities is entirely coincidental.

Pegasus Division is an imprint of Mark Wisnewski

First edition

ISBN: 978-1-7644073-2-8

This book was professionally typeset on Reedsy.
Find out more at reedsy.com

For the ones who came home changed, and the hearts that waited anyway.

"Some hearts never stop fighting. They just change what they're fighting for."

- Jackson "Jax" Wilder
Staff Sgt, Pegasus Special Security

Contents

Foreword

Every story starts with a choice—fight, or walk away.

For the men and women of Pegasus Special Security, walking away was never an option.

Born from the wreckage of battles no one remembers, Pegasus is built by soldiers who learned that not all wars are fought on foreign soil. Some happen inside the heart. They protect what can't be replaced. Families, secrets, second chances and sometimes, the people they swore to forget.

These missions aren't about medals or orders. They're about redemption, loyalty, and the quiet kind of courage it takes to love again when everything else has burned down.

This is where their stories begin.

Where protection becomes personal, and danger starts to look a lot like desire.

Welcome to Pegasus.

The mission starts here.

— Stephanie Colson
For the brave, the broken, and those who still believe in love worth bleeding for.

Preface

Every story starts somewhere.

This one begins on Australia's Gold Coast, where the men and women of **Pegasus Special Security** guard what matters most—people. Not governments. Not corporations. Just lives worth saving.

They're fighters, healers, and survivors, each carrying the scars of battles both seen and unseen. And every mission will test not just their skill, but their capacity to love.

Savage Protector is the first step into that world—where protection comes before politics, redemption is the reward, and love is the vow that keeps them standing.

— *Stephanie Colson*

This story was written for anyone learning to trust again.

You can rebuild. You can fall in love again. You can begin.

_- SC

1

CHAPTER 1 - THE ROAD HOME

Crimson Creek, Queensland

The afternoon light hit the highway in dull, wavering sheets, the kind that made every kilometre feel like two. Jax Hart rolled his shoulders as he drove, the muscle through his back still tight from the last job, the one that had spat him out of the Northern Territory with a stitched arm, two cracked ribs, and a handler who'd said, "Take the week. Breathe. Or pretend you will."

He'd laughed at that.

Breathing wasn't his strong suit lately.

The Pegasus-issued ute hummed beneath him, tyres thudding rhythmically over the patched bitumen. A battle-scarred esky rattled on the passenger seat, wedged between his pack and a bundle of cables he should've returned months ago. He passed the "Welcome to Crimson Creek" sign and felt something in his chest tighten the way it always did here — not pain, not dread. Something older. Heavier. A knot made of memory.

Home was the wrong word.

But this place had a claim on him all the same.

The road narrowed as it wound through the last few trees, eucalyptus leaves flashing silver in the wind. He lowered the window, letting the scent of dust and gum wash through the cabin. Magpies warbled somewhere above. A storm felt close, though the sky showed nothing but hard blue.

Classic Creek weather — pretending calm right before it broke.

He turned left at the roundabout, passing the Shell servo, the old hardware store with the peeling green paint, and the butcher whose chalkboard out front always looked like it had been written in a windstorm. The town felt the same. A little tired. A little stubborn. A place that didn't hurry for anyone.

He hadn't told anyone he was coming back.

No reason to.

He'd only intended to be here for a day. Two at most. Set up the Mill, check the equipment, update the failovers, and head out again before the town remembered to resent him.

But as he rolled down Main Street, he caught himself slowing. Something inside him knew—had always known—that there was one place he couldn't just drive past.

Red Wolf Books & Brew.

The café sat wedged between the old barber and the charity shop, its cream-painted timber glowing warm in the sun. The awning fluttered. A small chalkboard sign read: **Open Late — Try Our New Chai** with a crooked smiley face. The windows gleamed.

And behind one of them, for the first time in two years, he saw her.

Callie Frost.

She moved between tables with that same effortless grace she'd always had — not floaty, not shy. Just... grounded. Like her feet knew where to go before her mind did. Her blonde hair was tied back loosely, strands escaping to brush her cheek. She laughed at something an older man said, eyes crinkling at the corners.

Jax's hand tightened on the steering wheel.

He should keep driving.

He told himself that.

He'd said he wouldn't interfere. Wouldn't disturb the life she'd built in the ruins he'd left behind. He owed her space. A whole galaxy of space.

But his foot eased off the accelerator anyway.

He pulled into the parking bay across from the café and sat there a moment, watching. Breathing. Trying to decide if this was a mistake.

Then Callie turned toward the window.

And saw him.

Her whole body stilled.

Her smile faded.

Not anger.

Not joy.

Something tighter. Sharper. Like her breath caught on old scar tissue.

She taught him how to read that look once.

Two years hadn't made him forget.

A customer spoke to her. She nodded absently, murmured something, wiped her hands on her apron, and stepped through the back doorway out of sight.

He swore under his breath.

This was a mistake.

But he'd made a promise — to Maya, to Logan, to himself — that he'd check on this town, this outpost, this place that never seemed to stay quiet on the intel boards. And if checking on the town meant checking on her... that was just geography. Not an excuse.

He got out of the ute.

Heat hit him instantly — thick, humid, clinging. He crossed the street, each step heavier than the last, and reached the café door.

For a long second he didn't push it open.

Then he did.

A soft bell chimed overhead, the sound painfully familiar. The air inside was warm with coffee, cinnamon, and something citrusy he could never name. Timber floors creaked underfoot. Shelves of books lined the walls, spines mismatched and colourful.

Callie stood behind the counter, arms folded. Not defensive — bracing.

"Hey," she said.

Her voice was steady. Impressive.

His heart did something stupid.

"Hey," he replied, because eloquence had never been his skillset around her. "Place looks good."

"It should," she said. "I keep it alive. You know. Myself."

Right.

He deserved that.

Jax nodded once. "I'm not here to cause trouble."

"That's new," she said, a tiny spark of humour flickering through her eyes before she tamped it down.

He almost smiled. Almost.

"I'm in town overnight," he said. "Just checking systems at the Mill. Figured I..." He gestured vaguely, like a rookie. "Should say hi."

"You never figured that before."

Fair.

She sighed — not dramatically, just tiredly — and placed a mug under the machine, steam curling around her fingers.

"You want coffee?" she asked.

Professional. Polite. Distant.

He swallowed. "Yeah. Thanks."

She made it wordlessly, sliding the mug across the counter toward him. He watched her hands. They were steady, but her jaw wasn't. She was trying hard not to ask why he was really here.

Before he could speak, a man at the corner table raised his voice.

"Callie! That parcel guy's back."

She frowned. "Again? He was just here this morning."

"Dropped something on the step," the man said, squinting through the window. "Didn't knock this time."

Jax's pulse shifted.

He set the coffee down.

"Callie," he said quietly, "you expecting packages?"

"Always," she said, moving around the counter. "Books, beans, supplies—"

She opened the door and froze.

Something sat on the top step.

Small.

Wrapped in white butcher paper.

4

Tied with silver tape.

Her breath hitched — not panic, not yet, but recognition.

Jax stepped beside her. "You okay?"

"It's nothing," she said quickly. Too quickly. "Just a delivery."

"Callie."

She swallowed, eyes lingering on the parcel.

"This keeps happening," she admitted softly. "But it's probably a mix-up."

A lie.

He could hear it in her voice.

Jax bent down, gloved hand brushing the parcel—

—and the paper under his fingers shifted.

Something slid inside.

Something small.

Hard.

Metallic.

A key?

He peeled the tape, slow, careful.

Inside lay a single object:

A charm bracelet link.

A tiny wolf.

Callie inhaled sharply.

Jax looked at her.

Her eyes were glass-bright.

"That's mine," she whispered. "My mum gave it to me when I turned eighteen. But I—I lost it years ago."

He straightened. "Callie. Where exactly did you lose it?"

Her throat bobbed. "In the city. Before I moved here. I thought it fell off on a riverwalk. I never found it."

Jax's mind shifted gears — fast and lethal.

Someone had been close to her years ago.

Close enough to find what she lost.

Close enough to keep it.

The charm lay cold in his palm.

He glanced toward the road.

The courier bike was already gone.

Callie's voice cracked. "It's not... it can't be what it looks like."

But it was.

Every instinct in Jax's body snapped awake.

He looked at her and said quietly, with absolute clarity:

"Callie. Someone has been watching you for a very long time."

And the storm finally broke.

2

CHAPTER 2 - FAULT LINES

Pegasus Mill — After Dusk

The old warehouse stood against the dark like a ribcage—steel beams, century-old brick, windows reinforced with mesh. Jax unlocked the door, guided her through, and the generator hum rose like a heartbeat.

Screens flickered to life in the main room—street cams, door cams, the alley behind the café.

Her breath caught. "You've been watching my block?"

"Not officially," he said.

"Jax—"

"You weren't answering my messages."

Her heart stuttered. "What messages?"

He froze. "You didn't get them."

"No."

"What about calls?"

"None."

Something cold slid through him. "Then someone's intercepting."

✦ ✦ ✦

Logan appeared on the mezzanine, leaning on the rail. "Well, well. Look who dragged home trouble."

"Nice to see you too," Callie muttered.

"I didn't say it wasn't nice." Logan grinned. "Just chaotic."

Maya followed, tablet in hand, eyes sharp behind her glasses. "Callie. You okay?"

Callie managed a nod. "Working on it."

Maya shot Jax a look. "You told her yet?"

"Not everything," he said.

"Well, don't sugar-coat it. Whoever's watching her is escalating."

Callie went still. "Define escalating."

Maya switched on the main monitor. A grainy feed showed a figure standing in darkness near the café. Unmoving. Watching.

Callie's breath hitched. "Oh God."

Jax stepped beside her, voice soft. "You're not alone anymore."

"That's what scares me," she whispered.

✦ ✦ ✦

Later, when the others drifted off to their stations, Callie wandered toward the far corner, hands shaking. Jax followed without noise, giving her space until she spoke.

"When you left..." She swallowed. "I told myself you had your reasons."

"I did."

She met his gaze, raw. "But you broke something."

"I know."

"Do you regret it?"

"Every day."

The confession landed like a flare in the dark—brief, bright, dangerous.

"Jax..." she whispered.

"Callie." His voice dropped. "I'm here now. And I'm not leaving."

It shouldn't have steadied her.

It did.

3

CHAPTER 3 - FORCED PROXIMITY

Crimson Creek, Queensland — Red Wolf Books & Brew

For a second they just stared at the tiny metal wolf in his palm.

It didn't look like much.

Just a charm dangling from a short section of broken link, silver dulled at the edges where years had rubbed it soft.

But Callie was looking at it like it was a fingerprint pressed straight into her chest.

"That's—" Her voice caught. She swallowed and tried again. "That's mine."

Jax kept his tone level. "You're sure?"

"Jax." She lifted her hand, fingers trembling. "I wore it every day from eighteen to twenty-four. I used to twist it when I was nervous. Mum said it suited me. 'Little wolf-girl', she'd say. It fell off on the riverwalk after work one night. I went back the next morning. It was gone."

"Where was this?" he asked.

"Brisbane." Her eyes didn't leave the charm. "Two years before I moved here."

He let that land, clean and brutal. "So it vanished in the city. And turned up today on your doorstep. In hand-delivered packaging."

A muscle jumped in her jaw. "People lose things and find them again.

Maybe someone—"

"You don't believe that," he said quietly.

Her shoulders slumped. "No."

A customer cleared his throat near the back, the scrape of a chair reminding them they weren't alone. Callie stepped back into the doorway, the reflexive host.

"I'll be with you in a sec, Mrs Keegan," she called, voice almost normal.

"Take your time, love," came the answer. "Just admiring your display."

Jax closed his fingers around the charm. "How many of these packages have you had?"

She hesitated. "A few."

"How many, Callie?"

"Six," she said finally. "Maybe seven."

His pulse ticked up. "And you didn't think to mention this to anyone?"

"I mentioned it to my diary," she said, brittle. "And to the bin. Look, it's not like they've all been creepy."

"Show me."

She almost said no. He saw it. The reflex to handle it herself, to prove she didn't need anyone. Especially him.

Then another part of her — the part that had always been too honest for her own good — won.

"Give me five minutes," she said. "I'll grab the box."

She slipped inside. The bell chimed as the door shut behind her, leaving him on the step with the weight of the tiny wolf in his hand.

He scanned the street out of habit. A mum wrangling a pram. Two teenagers sharing chips on the low wall by the post office. A council worker fiddling with the parking meter across the road. Nobody lingering. Nobody watching too long.

But whoever had wrapped that charm had been close enough to touch her once, in another life.

And close enough to find her again.

He pocketed the wolf and followed her inside.

✦ ✦ ✦

She met him by the staff door with a shoebox that had once held boots and now held something much stranger.

"Office," he said. "Back, away from the windows."

She nodded, jaw tight, and led the way through the narrow service corridor past the sinks and stock cupboard. The small room out the back smelled of cardboard and lemon cleaner. A desk, a filing cabinet, a pinboard full of invoices and scribbled notes.

She set the box down like it might explode.

Inside, nestling in white paper like a collection of tiny, private crimes:

A ribbon from one of her old city gift bags, tied in the exact same knot she used to make.

A cafe loyalty card from a Brisbane espresso bar, every square punched except the last one.

A single Polaroid of the riverwalk at dusk. The angle was familiar. Her favourite bench in the background. No people. Just space where she used to sit.

A red pen. Same brand she'd used at her old job. The nib was chewed the way she used to chew it.

And three scraps of card, each about the size of a business card, each with two words in the same careful, blocky handwriting.

Still watching.

Still here.

Still yours.

No threats. No demands. No name.

Just possessive little ghosts.

Jax felt the back of his neck go hot.

"How long?" he asked.

She leaned against the desk, arms folded tight over her chest. "First one arrived three months ago. The ribbon. No note. I thought someone was playing a joke. Then the coffee card. Then the Polaroid with 'Still watching.'"

"And you didn't tell anyone?"

"Tell who?" Her voice sharpened. "The local cops who still call my café 'the bookshop' because they can't be bothered remembering the actual name? The girls at yoga? 'Hey, funny story, someone's mining my past for souvenirs and hand-delivering them'? That doesn't sound crazy at all."

"You could've called me," he said before he could stop himself.

Her eyes flashed. "No, Jax. I couldn't."

Right. That one was on him.

He blew out a slow breath. "What about neighbours? Any of them seen the drop-offs?"

"Mrs Keegan mentioned a courier van a few times. Box on the step, no knock. And Noah from down the street—" She cut herself off.

"What about Noah?" Jax asked.

"He's a tradie," she said quickly. "Helps with the odd fix when I can't get someone official. He just said, 'Nice someone's thinking of you.'" Her mouth twisted. "Like I needed that."

He studied the items again. "Any of this ever shows up inside? Not just at the door?"

She looked away. "The pen did. I found it on my counter one morning, weighted on top of the eftpos Z-report. I thought I'd just misplaced it. Until the same thing happened with one of the little sugar spoons. And a napkin folded like the ones I used to do at Trident. But maybe that's nothing. Maybe I'm seeing patterns."

He shook his head. "You're not."

"You don't know that."

"I know people like this," he said, tone gone flat. "They like rituals. They like souvenirs. They like feeling clever. They especially like being the only one who knows the whole story."

Her fingers tightened on her arms. "You think it's him."

"Who?" he asked, though he already knew.

Her gaze flickered to the shoebox. "Evan."

The name shivered through the room.

"Tell me," he said.

"Nothing to tell," she lied.

"Callie."

She shut her eyes for a moment. When she opened them again, the edges were sharper. "He was my boss at Trident Media. Smart. Charming. Everyone loved him. He picked favourites. I was one for a while."

"How long?"

"A year. I thought he was mentoring me. Turned out he was keeping me off-balance. Little comments. Little demands. 'Wear your hair down for this client, they like friendly.' 'Stay late, you're better with the numbers.' It never crossed a line you could photograph. It just..." She rubbed her collarbone. "Got under my skin."

"Did he ever show up uninvited?"

"Once. Outside my flat. Said he was 'checking I got home safe.'" Her mouth curled. "After he'd worked me till midnight."

"Any gifts?"

"A few," she said, almost shrugging. "A book on running your own business. A scarf. A framed print I never hung. I left most of it when I moved."

"And when you stopped playing along?"

"He didn't like that." Her laugh came out brittle. "He switched me to the accounts no one wanted. Got someone else to make my old coffees. Stopped speaking to me if he could help it. Except when he needed something. When I handed in my resignation, he said..." Her throat worked. "'You'll be back. Nobody leaves me for long.'"

Jax felt a familiar surge of rage, cold and clean. "You get an AVO?"

"I looked into it," she said. "The forms, the appointments, the questions that make it sound like your fault. In the end, I thought, if I'm gone, I'm gone. I blocked his number. Deleted the emails. Moved three hundred kilometres south and changed my life."

"And he just let you go?"

"He sent three 'I'm worried' emails I didn't answer. One voicemail where he sounded really hurt. Then nothing." Her lips pressed together. "For a while I thought maybe I was the one being dramatic."

He nodded at the box. "And now?"

"Now I think maybe he rearranged the drama." She wrapped her hands around herself. "But it's been two years, Jax. Two. Why now?"

"Men like him don't let go of their favourite stories," he said. "Maybe he got bored. Maybe something in his life changed. Maybe he saw a photo of your café. Maybe he tripped over one memory too many and it woke him up. It doesn't matter why." His voice gentled. "What matters is we treat this for what it is. Stalking. Escalating."

Her eyes went to the scrap that read Still here.

"Escalating to what?" she whispered.

"Something we stop," he said simply.

The bell out front chimed again. Callie straightened instinctively.

"I have to—"

"I've got it," he said. "You... breathe. I'll cover the floor for five."

She blinked. "You, behind my counter?"

He shrugged. "How hard can it be?"

She huffed despite herself. "Famous last words."

✦ ✦ ✦

He did not, as it turned out, cover the floor.

He hovered near the espresso machine while she took orders, slipping back into the role she knew best. He watched the street like a second set of windows. Every time a van slowed, his hand twitched toward his phone. No one left anything this time. No more packages. No more charms.

Just an ordinary run of ordinary people with ordinary caffeine needs.

By late afternoon, the sky had gone from hard blue to a washed-out, unsettled grey. The wind picked up, rattling the awning. Somewhere over the hills, thunder muttered.

"Storm coming," Mrs Keegan said as she collected her takeaway chai. "Good for the gardens, bad for the powerlines."

"Backup generator at the Mill's ready," Jax said automatically.

Mrs Keegan smiled. "Of course it is, love. You Pegasus folk think of everything."

14

Callie slid another tray of muffins into the glass case. "You really set up in the old sawmill?"

"We liked the bones," he said. "Strong foundations. Few windows."

"Romantic," she said.

He allowed the ghost of a smile. "Functional."

The afternoon crowd thinned. The storm drew closer, the sky bruising at the edges. The scent of rain pushed in whenever the door opened, sharp and metallic.

At five-fifteen, a courier van rolled slowly down the street. White, nondescript, one of a dozen that passed through every week. It didn't stop. Just cruised by, wipers squeaking.

Callie still flinched.

Logan picked up on the second ring.

"Tell me you're calling to say the coffee's good," he said by way of greeting.

"Coffee's good," Jax said, watching the van disappear. "Also, we've got a situation."

"Of course we do." Logan's tone shifted instantly, easy humour flattening into focus. "Talk to me."

He gave him the short version — the charm, the box, the notes, Evan's name.

Logan whistled. "And here I was thinking your hometown trip might actually be restful."

"Do I look like I make restful choices?"

"Fair. You secure the site?"

"Not yet. I'm still visible. I don't want him spooked into shadow. We need to parse whether this is long-distance puppet-mastering or someone local running his script."

"Copy," Logan said. "You're at the café till close?"

"Yeah. Rain's coming in. If he's been using deliveries as cover, he might like the anonymity."

"I'll run Pierce through the network, see if his name's left a digital smear near here. Maya's on shift; she'll love this."

"Tell Maya to be gentle with the victim," Jax said, glancing at Callie wiping

15

the counter like she could erase the last hour. "She's done her own risk assessments, but nobody's taken her seriously yet. We change that."

"Roger that. Tell Callie the Pegasus cavalry says hi."

"Logan—"

"I know," Logan said. "I'll play it quiet. Keep me posted if anything goes boom. Or clinks. Or creaks suspiciously."

Jax hung up and slid the phone back into his pocket.

"Pegasus?" Callie asked, not quite looking at him.

"Logan," he said. "He'll run your ex. See if any of this matches other cases."

She poured milk into a jug, eyes on the swirl. "You think I'm just one of his cases now?"

"No." He watched her work, the concentration smoothing the lines around her mouth. "You're one of mine."

The answer came out too easily. Too true.

She blinked hard and set the jug down before she overfilled it. "We close in an hour."

"Good," he said. "Then we talk about tonight."

"Tonight?"

"The bricks and mortar here are cute," he said, glancing at the windows. "They won't stop a determined man. The Mill will. You're not sleeping above this shop while someone's playing postman."

She bristled instantly. "I'm not hiding."

"I didn't say hide," he said. "I said move. Temporarily. Controlled environment, better camera angles, fewer access points. You can open in the morning if nothing happens. But tonight, you're with me."

"Wow," she said. "You practice that commanding tone in the mirror or you just born with it?"

"A little from column A," he said dryly. "But I'm right."

She hated that he was. She hated that the idea of sleeping above the café with those notes in a shoebox made her skin crawl. She hated that the only place her nervous system seemed to unclench lately was in motion.

"Doesn't feel fair," she muttered, wiping an imaginary smear.

"Fair's not on the menu," he said gently. "Survival is."

She leaned on the counter with both hands, head bowed for a second. When she looked up, her eyes were tired but clear.

"Fine," she said. "Mill sleepover. But if you snore, I'm pushing you off the mezzanine."

"Deal," he said.

The bell chimed again. A guy in a hi-vis shirt ordered a flat white and left his change in the tip jar with a wink. Outside, the clouds finally broke. Rain came down in sudden, heavy sheets, turning the street into a river of reflected light.

"See?" Mrs Keegan said on her way past the window. "Told you. Good for the gardens."

Lightning flashed, turning the café white for a heartbeat. Thunder followed a few seconds later, a deep rolling growl that made the windows hum.

Callie glanced instinctively at the door, then at him. "You ever get tired of being right about storms?"

He shook his head. "Storms are honest. People, not so much."

✦ ✦ ✦

They closed early.

The storm had gone from dramatic to dangerous, wind knifing down the street, rain coming at the windows sideways. The power flickered twice, long enough for someone at the back to say, "Oh, not again," and for Callie's stomach to turn.

"Alright, folks," she said, putting on her best customer voice. "We're calling it. I love you all but not enough to be responsible for broken necks on wet footpaths. Last coffees on the house — take them and run."

They laughed, grateful. Cups were filled, lids snapped on, goodnights exchanged. Within fifteen minutes the café was empty except for them.

Jax dragged the metal security grille down over the glass, the rattle and clank loud over the storm. Callie wiped the last of the crumbs from the counter and killed the front lights, leaving only the warm glow over the

17

register.

"Feels wrong," she said softly, looking at the darkened room. "Like I've put it to bed sick."

"It'll wake up," he said.

She grabbed a small overnight bag from behind the counter, already half-packed — jeans, tee, underwear. She hadn't decided to go with him when she stuffed it earlier, but some part of her must have known which way the scales would tip.

"Give me two minutes upstairs," she said. "Brush teeth, grab my laptop, tell the plants not to die of abandonment. Then we go."

"I'll wait here," he said.

She hesitated. "You sure?"

If she meant, You're not coming up to check my flat? he heard it.

"Door stays in my line of sight," he said. "You scream, I run. That work?"

Her mouth twitched. "You always did have a way with reassurance."

She disappeared up the back stairs, keys jingling. He listened to her footsteps overhead — crossing, pausing, moving again. Water drummed on the roof, wind moaning down the alley.

He checked the front lock twice, then moved behind the counter to test the back door, touching each point of security like beads on a rosary. He'd just finished when the first crash came.

Glass breaking.

Sharp. Sudden. Too close.

"Callie!"

"I'm okay!" Her voice came from above, slightly breathless. "That was upstairs—"

Another crash cut her off.

This one was downstairs.

He was moving before the sound finished, gun out, body between the front windows and the rest of the shop. The security grille had held, but a spiderweb of cracks spread across the right-hand pane. In the middle of the pattern, something heavy rested against the glass.

A brick.

Wrapped in paper.

Crimson ink bleeding where the rain found it.

He edged closer.

The word was half-washed away but still readable, the letters big and deliberate.

MINE.

Thunder rolled over the roof like applause.

He holstered the weapon long enough to catch the brick in both hands as another gust rattled the grille. Up close, he could see the edges of the paper had been folded with absurd care, corners neat, tape pressed flush. As if whoever had wrapped it thought they were leaving a gift.

Callie stopped halfway down the stairs, one hand clamped white on the rail.

"Jax—"

"I've got it," he said. "Stay back."

She came anyway, slow and stunned, until she could see the word.

Her breath left her in a sound that wasn't quite a sob. "He wouldn't—"

"He just did," Jax said.

Rain sneaked through the broken pane in silver threads. A few shards dropped and shattered on the hardwood. The storm howled round the awning like something with teeth.

He carried the brick to the counter, setting it carefully on a stainless tray. The red ink had smeared under his fingers, streaking the M like a wound.

"What does he want?" she whispered.

"Control," Jax said. "Fear. Your attention." He met her eyes. "He doesn't get the first two. The last one we decide."

Her chin lifted a fraction. "Then I decide he only gets it on my terms."

He almost smiled. "That's my girl."

The words slipped out before he could catch them.

Heat flared in her cheeks — anger, memory, something else.

"Not your girl," she said automatically, but her voice shook less than it had a minute ago.

"Fine," he said. "Then you're Red Wolf. And Red Wolf isn't staying here tonight."

She nodded once, sharp. "Okay. Mill it is."

He pulled his phone one-handed, already snapping photos — brick, word, glass pattern, outside street. He caught the dark blur of a hatchback disappearing around the corner, too far to get plates.

"Logan," he said when the call connected. "We've got escalation. Brick at the window, crimson MINE on the paper."

Logan swore softly. "Any eyes on the thrower?"

"Just a tail-light ghosted in the rain. Probably local, knows the streets."

"I'll pull the closest council cams," Logan said. "Maya's already in a mood about Pierce, this'll cheer her right up."

"Tell her to be nice," Jax said. "Callie's coming to the Mill."

"Copy that. I'll warm the generator and hide the good biscuits."

He cut the call and turned back to her. She was staring at the broken pane like if she concentrated hard enough she could put it back together.

"Callie," he said gently.

She blinked and looked at him.

"You with me?"

"Yeah." Her throat bobbed. "Yeah. Just... adjusting to the décor."

"Brick chic's not your look," he said. "Grab whatever you need for the night. We're not coming back until we've got better locks and better cameras."

She gave a short, strangled laugh. "You realise I own this place, right? I can't exactly announce a stalking season to the regulars."

"Then we solve it before they ever know," he said. "Best kind of security— quiet."

She ran a hand through her hair, took a breath that shuddered in the middle, and straightened. "Two minutes."

He watched her go up the stairs again, this time listening harder, muscles coiled. The storm battered the front windows, rain blowing through the gap like a hissed warning. He checked the grille again — solid. He checked the back door — locked. He checked his weapon — ready.

Callie came down faster than before, overnight bag over her shoulder, laptop bag cross-body, keys clinking.

She paused at the counter long enough to look at the brick again.

"He really wrote it, didn't he?" she said. "Mine. Like I'm a coffee mug he left in the staff kitchen."

"You're not his anything," Jax said.

She reached out and, with one decisive swipe of her thumb, smeared the last clear letter until the word blurred beyond reading.

"Good," she said. "Then he can learn to spell 'No' next."

The drive to the Mill took six minutes in good weather.

Tonight, with the storm flinging water sideways and the gutters trying to drown the road, it took ten. Ten long minutes where every pair of headlights behind them felt like a tail and every flash of lightning lit up a possible threat.

Callie sat with both hands wrapped around the strap of her bag, knuckles white. The café receded in the rearview, a soft square of yellow swallowed by rain.

"You sure it's secure?" she asked, voice lost under a rumble of thunder.

"Mill's a bunker," he said. "Steel bones, single bay, cameras on all sides. We use it for ops that need containment."

"Containment," she repeated. "Great. Very reassuring."

"It is," he said. "Because if he tries anything there, he stops being a ghost."

She looked at him sideways. "You ever scared?"

"Of storms?" he deflected.

"Of anything."

"Sure," he said. "All the time."

Her brows rose. "Liar."

"I'm scared of failing people who trusted me," he said, eyes on the windscreen. "Scared of not getting there in time. Scared of missing the detail that mattered."

"And me?"

He glanced at her. "You're not a fear. You're a responsibility I walked away from once. I don't intend to repeat that."

The air between them shifted, tight and hot and fragile.

She looked out at the rainy blur. "You left for good reasons."

"I left," he said simply. "Good reasons don't change the fact you stood there watching me go."

"Don't," she whispered. "Not now."

"Okay," he said. "Not now."

The Mill rose out of the rain like some rusted ship run aground — old sawtooth roof, corrugated iron walls, Pegasus logo small and discreet near the personnel door. He pulled into the bay, killed the engine, and listened. Just rain on steel. Wind at the eaves. No other cars.

"Stay in the ute," he said. "I'll open up."

He sprinted to the side door, key in, alarm off, lights on in a sequence his muscles knew better than most prayers. The generator growled awake. Security monitors flickered to life, painting the mezzanine in ghostly blues.

He jogged back, opened her door. "Come on, Red Wolf."

She slid down, landing in a puddle that splashed her ankle. "Ugh. Perfect."

"Consider it your baptism into witness protection," he said.

"Don't joke," she muttered, but the edge in her tone had dulled a fraction.

Inside, the Mill felt exactly as he'd promised: functional. Honest. High ceilings criss-crossed by steel beams, mezzanine office running along one side, workbenches and storage on the floor below. The air smelled of oil and dust and the ghost of cut timber.

He locked the door behind them, dropping three heavy bolts into place, each chunk of metal into steel a small, solid promise. The storm's howl dulled to a muffled roar, like the wind had its face pressed up against glass and couldn't quite get in.

Callie stepped to the middle of the open floor, turning slowly.

"It smells like salt and ghosts," she said.

"That's the sea," he said. "And maybe the past."

"You always talk in riddles," she said, but there was a corner of a smile with it now. "Or is that a Pegasus thing?"

"It's a 'trying not to say the wrong thing' thing."

"Then you're halfway there."

The generator coughed, then settled into a steady hum. The monitors above them showed four squares of rain-slicked town, the café among them — dark, locked, alone.

Jax gestured to the far corner of the mezzanine where a small cluster of cots and a portable heater sat. "Refuge central. You get the one near the heater. Fresh blanket. I'll sit watch."

"You ever actually rest?" she asked.

"Sometimes I blink slow."

"That doesn't count."

He shrugged. "It does for me."

She climbed the metal stairs, footsteps echoing, and dropped her bag beside the nearest cot. From up there, the whole Mill lay at her feet — workbenches, tool racks, the wide open bay, the river of cables running from the generator to the monitor bank like veins.

She looked small in the vastness, he thought. But not fragile. Like a match you could build a fire around if you were careful.

He joined her, handing over a folded blanket and a bottle of water. "You can write down everything that's happened, if it helps," he said. "Details matter."

She pulled a small notebook from her bag and rolled a pencil between her fingers. "It's not just for you," she said. "It's proof. If I write the day down, it means it actually happened. Not just in my head."

"Sometimes that's enough," he said.

She sat on the edge of the cot, notebook open on her knees. The first lines formed under her hand, slow and deliberate. Outside, lightning flickered through the grimy skylights, silvering the air.

"Jax," she said softly.

He looked up.

"Last time you said 'It'll be okay'..." Her eyes met his, clear and tired and something else. "Were you lying then?"

His throat worked. "No," he said. "I just didn't add 'eventually.'"

Her laugh was small but real. "I can live with eventually."

He leaned against the desk beside her, the warmth from the heater reaching his boots, the storm wrapping itself around the Mill in long, low sounds.

For the first time since he'd driven into Crimson Creek, the world felt like it might exhale.

◆ ◆ ◆

Hours later, after she'd drifted to a shallow, stubborn sleep and he'd walked every perimeter twice, the Mill settled into its storm rhythm — creaks finding a pattern, wind pushing breath through old seams.

He was at the railing when he heard it.

A clean, deliberate clink.

Metal on metal.

Not wind.

Not building.

He froze, listening. The sound came again, softer. A faint scrape under the rain, like someone testing a latch that wasn't theirs.

He reached for the weapon on the chair beside him.

"Callie," he said quietly.

Her eyes opened at once — the kind of sleep that never quite lets go. "What?"

"Stay there."

She listened. Heard it too. The scrape. The whisper of pressure where there shouldn't be any.

Her hand found the edge of the blanket. "Footsteps?"

"Metal shift," he murmured. "Tool bench maybe. Or the hatch."

The storm growled overhead. The generator's hum felt suddenly too loud, like it might give away their breathing.

He moved down the stairs with practiced quiet, hand grazing the railing only where it wouldn't groan. At the bottom, the air was colder, close to the concrete, the night pressing against the walls.

The workbench sat where he'd left it. The main door was locked, bolts seated. But at the small service hatch near the loading dock, the handle

24

twitched.

A soft metallic rattle. Quick. Contained.

"Who's there?" he called, voice level.

Silence.

Then the sound of a breath held too long.

Then footsteps retreating, quick and light.

He threw the latch and yanked the hatch open. The yard outside lay empty, puddles rippling under the rain. But on the concrete lip, just inside the line where weather stopped and shelter began, were two wet prints.

Trainers.

One set heavier.

One set light.

He stepped out into the rain, letting it soak his shirt in seconds, scanning the fence line. The chain-link sagged under wet vines, the shadows beyond thick. Whoever had been there was gone.

Or very good at being unseen.

When he came back up the stairs, water dripping from his hair, Callie was on her feet, blanket around her shoulders like a cloak.

"Anyone?" she asked.

"Not now," he said. "But they were."

Her face went pale under the harsh light. "How would he know we came here?"

"He shouldn't." Jax scrubbed a hand over his face. "Unless he's been mapping every place I'd take you."

"Can he do that?"

"Men like him don't need to be right," he said. "They just need to feel close." He glanced at the cameras. The café feed showed only the quiet dark. For now. "He's testing boundaries. Finding his stage."

She sank back onto the cot, notebook forgotten. "And what do we do?"

"We hold," he said. "We watch back. And we make it very clear he picked the wrong town."

Lightning flashed again, washing the room white. When it faded, Callie was still there. Breathing. Upright. Alive.

Red Wolf in a steel den, with the storm clawing at the walls and a man somewhere out there thinking she was his.

Jax sat across from her, back to the monitors, eyes steady on hers.

"He doesn't get to write this story," he said.

Her mouth curved, a faint, fierce thing. "Good," she said. "I always preferred editing."

Outside, the storm dug in.

Inside, the first real line of defence drew itself between them and the dark.

4

CHAPTER 4 - STORM FRONT

Crimson Creek — Before Dawn

The sky hadn't quite made up its mind yet — not night, not morning, a bruised blue-grey caught between breaths. The kind of light that made the whole town feel suspended, waiting for someone to move first.

Callie sat curled on the cot in the Mill, knees drawn up, a blanket pooled around her hips. Sleep had come in thin snatches, hard and shallow, peeling away at every small sound as if the night had teeth. Jax had slept less. She could tell by the way his shoulders held tension now, as if the weight of the dark hadn't quite lifted.

The generator hummed beneath the floorboards — steady, familiar, grounding. An anchor against the storm that seemed determined to bend her in half.

On the bench between them lay the charm link — that tiny wolf, silver dull from years spent in someone else's pocket. Callie stared at it like it was alive.

"I don't understand," she whispered.

Jax didn't sit. He paced in slow, controlled strides, processing the evidence board on the wall though he already knew every detail on it by heart.

"Someone kept that charm," he said. "Not by accident."

"I lost it near the Story Bridge. I remember that day. It fell off somewhere between the riverwalk and the steps."

"That man today didn't find it by luck."

She swallowed, voice thin. "It's been years. Whoever kept it... why bring it back now? Why here?"

He didn't answer right away. Not because he didn't know — but because saying it aloud made it real.

"You built a quiet life here," he said finally. "Small town. Predictable hours. Easy to watch." His jaw tightened. "It wouldn't take much for someone with an obsession to map your whole routine."

Her breath shuddered. "You think he followed me from the city?"

"Maybe." He rubbed the back of his neck. "Or he never stopped looking."

Silence stretched, taut as wire.

Callie folded her arms tight over her ribs, suddenly cold. "You think it's Evan."

"I think Evan Pierce is in the running," Jax said bluntly. "But the parcel guy today didn't move like a planner. He moved like a pawn."

She let out a rough, humourless laugh. "A stalker with staff."

He didn't smile. "Obsession breeds helpers. Copycats. Men who think they're protecting a woman who never asked them to."

She rubbed her face with both hands. "Maybe I shouldn't have come here."

"No," he said quietly. "The one who's wrong is the one watching you. Not you. Never you."

Her throat tightened painfully. "You sound sure."

"I am."

That surprised her. Not the certainty — Jax always spoke like the ground beneath him was a map only he could see — but the softness inside it.

She pushed up from the cot, wrapping her blanket around her. "I need coffee."

"Sit," he said gently. "I'll make it."

"Since when do you make coffee?"

"Since right now. Since you look like your bones forgot to hold you upright."

Something hot and unsteady pressed behind her ribs.

She sat.

28

He worked with quiet efficiency — filling the filter, warming the pot, flicking a switch with that same controlled precision he applied to everything else. The air filled with warmth and something like normality.

When he set the mug in front of her, she wrapped her hands around it like an anchor.

"Thanks."

"You're welcome."

She sipped. "Better than yours usually is."

He huffed a low sound — the ghost of a laugh.

Her eyes lifted to his. "What's the plan now?"

"Logan and Maya will run the street cams. Chase will sweep the rail-yard. I'll stay with you."

She nodded slowly, absorbing that. "All day?"

His voice didn't waver. "However long you need."

Her heart tripped over itself. "Jax... you don't have to—"

"Yes," he said, quiet but absolute. "I do."

Something inside her cracked open — not fear, not pain. Something warmer. Something terrifying in its own way.

She stared at her mug. "I don't want to be a burden."

"You aren't."

He said it like a fact, not reassurance.

"You never were."

She breathed in sharply.

He breathed out slowly.

The wolf charm glinted in a thin stripe of morning light.

✦ ✦ ✦

Crimson Creek — Mid-Morning

The town looked harmless again — the cruel kind of harmless that only small places could get away with. People wandered along the footpath, laughing, carrying bags of bread and fruit, greeting each other as if the world wasn't bending in on itself.

The illusion broke for Callie the second she pushed open the café door.

Everything familiar felt sharper.

The bell chimed too loud.

The windows glowed too bright.

Her reflection looked like she'd forgotten how to hide.

Jax followed her in, toolbox slung in one hand, scanning the street behind them with casual precision.

"Logan's ten minutes out," he murmured. "Maya says no sedan yet. No parcel bikes."

"Good," Callie said, though her heart thrashed anyway.

She flipped the sign to OPEN and tried to breathe like she wasn't a rabbit crawling out of a snare.

The morning warmed.

Cups clinked.

Milk steamed.

People filtered in, unaware of how close danger hovered.

Jax took a seat near the window, laptop open, eyes always moving.

Callie found her rhythm slowly — tamp, pull, pour, smile — each movement reminding her she still owned this place, even if a stranger thought otherwise.

Just before ten, a shadow slid across the doorway.

A woman stepped inside — tall, denim jacket, hair tied back in a loose knot, boots that whispered road dust. She carried a recorder but held it face-down.

"Hey," the woman said with easy confidence. "You must be Callie. I'm Mara Bell."

Conversation stilled for a second — the way it does when someone arrives with a different kind of energy.

Callie blinked. "Sorry—who?"

"Mara Bell," she repeated, offering a card. *Cold Case // Warm Hands — Podcast.* "I heard Crimson Creek has a story breathing heavier than most. Before you panic — I'm not here to make a circus."

Callie's shoulders stiffened. "We serve coffee. Not stories."

"Good," Mara said. "Then this will be short."

Jax stood instantly, subtle but unmistakable, shifting his weight like a man ready to intercept.

Mara's gaze flicked to him — quick assessment — then back to Callie.

"Off the record," she said. "Everything stays off the record unless you say otherwise. But..." She slid an envelope from her tote. "I want to show you something before someone else weaponises it."

She laid a photo on the counter.

Callie's stomach dropped.

The image was grainy, taken outside a high-rise in the city. Callie stood near the edge of the shot — younger, hair shorter, smile polite and strained. Beside her was a man with a neat beard and a hand hovering too close to her shoulder.

Evan Pierce.

Her ex-boss.

Her old nightmare.

Callie whispered, "Where did you get that?"

Mara shrugged. "Friend in the city press. I asked for shots outside Trident Media from the year you left. He showed up in half a dozen frames. So did you."

Jax moved beside her, body shifting into a different kind of readiness. "What's your angle?"

"Context," Mara said, calm but not unkind. "Predators hide in silence. I prefer noise."

Callie's voice cracked. "He's not here. He can't be."

"Maybe," Mara said. "But his pattern? It's showing up in someone else."

The coffee machine hissed like a warning.

Jax stepped in, voice dropping. "This conversation's over."

"Your call," Mara said, pocketing the photo. "If you decide to talk, I'll listen. On your terms."

She turned to leave, then paused. "For what it's worth—you look like someone who learned to survive. He won't like that."

The door chimed. She was gone.

31

Callie gripped the counter, knuckles white.

Jax's voice softened. "You okay?"

"No," she whispered. Then steadier: "But I will be."

Her phone buzzed.

Unknown number.

Twice.

She ignored it.

The bell chimed again.

Noah Briggs walked in — toolbox in hand, smile harmless, eyes too bright.

"Morning, Cal," he said. "Heard about your window. Thought I'd fix it."

Jax stepped forward. "We're covered."

Noah's smile thinned. "Didn't ask you."

"Not your place to," Jax replied.

Callie forced a polite tone. "Another time, Noah. Really."

He hesitated, jaw flexing, then nodded slowly and left — the bell chiming after him like something breaking.

Callie exhaled shakily.

Jax's eyes followed Noah's ute until it vanished around the corner.

"Stay visible," he murmured.

"I plan to."

But her phone buzzed again.

A message.

A draft she'd begun, cursor blinking.

I think I know —

She didn't remember typing it.

A chill slid down her spine.

And the day shifted.

CHAPTER 5— FRACTURE POINT

Crimson Creek — 11:22 a.m.

The bell over the café door had stopped swinging.

That was the first sign something was wrong.

Jax didn't know how long he'd been staring at Callie's abandoned phone — screen lit, message half-typed — before the silence got under his skin. A silence too clean. Too perfect. The kind that only existed right after the world had been scooped out.

He whispered her name once.

No answer.

He scanned the café.

Two customers chatting.

One mum pushing a pram.

Everything ordinary.

Except Callie was gone.

His pulse sharpened.

She'd told him she was stepping next door.

Two minutes.

That was nine minutes ago.

He pressed the comm in his ear.

Low, controlled. "Pegasus One to base. Callie's missing. Last contact: her phone. Last typed message: *I think I know—*"

Logan's voice hit immediately. "Lock down the block. I'm two minutes out."

Maya came through next — crisp, focused. "Triangulating her smartwatch... okay—got something. Moving signal. South-west. Rail-yard periphery. Four blocks."

Jax was already moving.

He grabbed her phone, shoved it into his pocket, and pushed out the café door.

Sunlight hit him like a physical thing.

The street shimmered in the heat.

Cars rolled past, blissfully unaware they were rolling over a crime scene.

His ute roared to life before he finished closing the door.

Hold on, Cal.

Gravel spat behind him as he tore through town, weaving around a school bus, cutting down Hutchison Street, engine growling low and deadly.

Maya's voice returned through static.

"Signal's almost stationary... warehouse cluster... number four—she's in Warehouse Four."

"Copy," he muttered. "Going in hot."

"Jax—don't breach blind—"

But he'd already killed the engine.

The old rail-yard loomed ahead — rusted metal, peeling signs, a skeleton of the Creek's industrial past. The air smelled like oil and sunburned steel.

Callie's bag sat abandoned near the roller door, strap torn as if someone had ripped it from her shoulder.

His stomach went cold.

He drew his gun.

"Callie," he called softly. "I'm here. Answer me."

A sound floated out.

Small.

Weak.

A breath that wasn't breath.

"Jax?"

He moved.

Through the door.

Into the dark.

Light spilt through broken windows in white, dusty slices. The space was empty except for—

Her.

Callie sat slumped against the far wall, wrists loosely bound, hair fallen across her cheek. A red cut ran along her left cheekbone. Her chest rose too fast. Eyes wide, pupils blown.

He dropped to his knees beside her in an instant.

"Callie. Hey. Look at me."

Her breath hitched and she grabbed his shirt with both shaking hands, rope falling uselessly from her wrists.

"He was here," she whispered. "He was right here."

"Who?" His voice cracked on the word.

"I didn't see his face." Her voice broke. "He said—he said I don't look at him anymore."

Jax's heart stuttered.

"He left through the back," she said. "I heard tyres. He carved something—"

Her gaze slid past him to the wall.

Jax followed it.

And froze.

Words gouged deep into the metal wall, scratches fresh enough to curl paint:

SHE'S MINE

The air punched out of him.

"Logan, I've got her," he said into the comm, voice raw. "Warehouse Four. He's gone."

"On your six," Logan replied. "Chase is pulling cameras."

Callie leaned her forehead against Jax's shoulder, breath shaking uncontrollably. He slid an arm around her, holding her steady without pulling her

35

too tight.

"You're okay," he murmured. "I've got you."

"I thought—" She stopped, swallowing hard. "I thought he wasn't real."

"He's real," Jax said softly. "But he just made a mistake."

"What mistake?"

"He touched you in my town."

And something in Jax's voice made Callie look up — a sound she'd never heard before. Not rage. Not violence.

Vow.

He cut the rope with a quick, controlled motion and helped her stand. Her knees buckled once; he steadied her with a hand at her waist.

"Slow," he whispered. "One breath at a time."

She nodded, though her hands still shook.

Sirens echoed distantly — two units closing fast.

Jax looked at the carved words again, fury quiet and surgical behind his ribs.

Callie followed his gaze.

"He's not done," she whispered.

"No," Jax agreed. "He isn't."

"Then we stop him."

He looked at her — the fear, the fire, the fracture, the fight — all wrapped into one trembling, determined woman.

"Yes," he said. "We stop him."

Outside, the sirens grew louder.

Inside, Warehouse Four held its breath.

And the world shifted toward war.

6

CHAPTER 6 - GHOST ON THE WIRE

Crimson Creek, Queensland — 02:17 a.m., The Pegasus Mill

The clock on the far wall had stopped sometime around midnight, but the Mill never slept.

The generator hummed in the belly of the building, low and steady. The monitors bled pale light over the mezzanine, throwing Jax's shadow long across the concrete. The others had gone—Logan to his rented room above the Switchyard, Maya to the motel near the highway, Chase snoring into a beanbag in the corner with a laptop balanced on his chest.

Callie was in the cot room behind the thin dividing wall, the soft rise and fall of her breathing barely audible over the machines.

Jax sat alone at the desk that passed for command, elbows braced, hands wrapped around a mug gone cold. On the central monitor, the café feed showed a dark rectangle of glass and empty chairs. The word that had been etched and then scrubbed away from the window still lived in his memory: MINE.

The worst enemies were the ones who believed that word.

He pushed the mug aside. His forearm twinged as the bandage pulled; he ignored it. Quiet pressed in—thick, heavy, full of all the things he tried not to think about when the sun was up.

The comms panel flickered with a faint standby glow. Old habit had him reaching out, fingers tracing the worn edge of the mic, like a rosary for someone who'd forgotten how to pray.

"You're doing it again," Logan's voice said in his head—not hallucination, just memory. "Staring at ghosts on the wire, mate. Nothing there but static."

Jax exhaled slowly and, for once, let the ghosts come.

✦ ✦ ✦

The first time he'd walked into this building, the air had smelled of sawdust and disuse. The old owner had stood beside him, calloused hand stroking the doorframe like the flank of an old horse.

"She's solid," the bloke had said. "Needs work, but she's seen worse storms than you."

Jax had believed him. He'd signed the lease on the spot, turned the Mill into a Pegasus outpost with a couple of laptops, a second-hand generator, and the kind of stubbornness you only get when you've run out of other choices.

Back then, Callie had been three hours' drive away, sitting in a hospice room with her mother and a copy of some dog-eared poetry book. He'd told himself it was temporary. That he'd do one more deployment, fill the bank, come back and be the man she thought he was.

The lie had almost worked. For a while.

✦ ✦ ✦

He blinked, dragged his gaze back to the present. The monitors showed nothing but rain-slick streets, a stray cat investigating a rubbish bin, the empty shape of Red Wolf's awning. Safe. Boring. The way he liked his watch to be.

He told himself to get up, to check the locks again, maybe force three hours' sleep out of the narrow bunk in the storeroom. Instead, his eyes slid to the far left of the corkboard, where an old photo had been half-buried under maps and notes.

Callie, four years younger, hair shorter, standing behind her café counter in some generic city laneway. He'd taken it the day she signed the lease. She hadn't known; he'd snapped it on his phone while she laughed with the electrician, head tipped back, pure light. Later, when she caught him setting it as his lock screen, she'd rolled her eyes and called him a sap.

He'd never argued.

Now the printed version was pinned to the wall with a red thumbtack, corners curling. Beside it, his own file photo from his first Pegasus contract. Fresh-faced. Clean-shaven. Eyes that hadn't yet learned how to stay open and numb at the same time.

He remembered that day with unwelcome clarity.

Sydney — Four Years Earlier

The hospital room had been too warm. The air smelled of antiseptic and cheap flowers; the window overlooked a brick wall and a sliver of sky the colour of dirty cotton.

Callie's mum had been propped against pillows, face pale but eyes bright. The cannula taped crooked on the back of her hand made him wince; she had laughed at him for that.

"Of all the things to bother you," she'd said, voice thin but amused. "You've been shot at, Jaxon Hart. I've heard the stories. And it's the tape that gets you?"

He'd smiled, because she needed him to. "Bad tape is a crime, Mrs Frost."

"Ellen," she'd corrected. "If you're going to break my daughter's heart, you don't get to be formal."

He'd flinched, just a fraction. She'd seen it. Of course she had. The woman missed nothing.

Callie had sat in the chair by the bed, her hand wrapped around her mother's fingers. There were shadows under her eyes that hadn't been there six months earlier. Hair scraped into a knot. Jeans thrown on without thinking. The kind of tired that seeps into bone.

39

He'd loved her so much it scared him. Loved the way she kept standing up, the way she kept making bad news sound manageable to her mum, the way she could still find a joke in the worst week of their lives. Loved her enough that when the call came, he'd answered.

"Contract's live," his Pegasus handler had said over the phone. "We need you on the flight tomorrow. Six months, maybe nine. Rural ops, extraction work. Pays triple your last job."

He'd looked at Callie then, at the band of pale skin on her finger where she twisted an absent ring, at the way she leaned into the bed when her mum coughed, absorbing the shock like it was her own body. He'd thought about the bills piling up on the kitchen table, the broken gearbox in the ute they couldn't afford to fix, the way Ellen worried that her daughter would be left with nothing but grief and a mortgage.

"I can't leave now," he'd said.

"We both know you will," the handler had replied. "You always do when it counts."

Later, standing by the hospice window while the sky turned the colour of bad tea, Callie had pressed her forehead into his chest.

"You're really going," she'd whispered.

"If I don't, we lose the house," he'd said. "We lose... everything. I can send enough back to—"

"I don't care about the house," she'd said sharply, pulling back to look at him. Her eyes had been too bright. "I care about you being here when she—" Her voice broke. She swallowed. "When it gets bad. When it gets real."

He'd cupped her face in both hands, thumbs brushing the damp under her eyes. "It's already real, Cal. That's why I have to go."

She'd stared at him as if trying to memorise every line. "I told you I'd never forgive you if you left."

"I know."

"And?"

He'd forced the words past his teeth. "I'm going anyway."

Ellen had watched them from the bed with that strange, calm compassion some people develop when they stand too close to their own ending. When

Callie left the room to find a nurse, Ellen had beckoned him closer.

"You're doing what you think is right," she'd said, voice soft but steady. "That's the curse of good men. Sometimes it still hurts the people you love."

"I don't know how to do both," he'd admitted. "Be here and fix it."

"You can't fix this," she'd said. "You can only stand in it. Question is: are you brave enough to stand in the part where she hates you?"

He'd looked away. He'd always been good at fighting things he could see. Feelings weren't on that list.

"I don't want her to hate me," he'd said.

"That's not the point," Ellen had replied gently. "The point is that she will. For a while. And you have to love her enough to let her."

He hadn't been that brave. Not then.

So he'd done what he was good at—he'd run towards the danger he could name, and left her alone with the kind he couldn't.

The memory sat heavy on his chest now, years later, in a steel-ribbed Mill that smelled of oil and rain.

He rose, stretching stiffness from his legs, and crossed to the small kitchenette. The kettle whined as he ran water into it. His reflection in the window above the sink looked older than he felt—lines around the mouth, grey beginning at his temples, eyes that had watched too many people fight for their lives and lose.

The first Pegasus op after he left Callie had been in a floodplain an ocean away. A village cut off by rising water, a bridge gone, a convoy trapped on the wrong side. His team had been dropped by chopper into a world of brown water and floating debris.

They'd moved from rooftop to rooftop, hauling people up with ropes and harnesses, the rotor wash turning rain into knives. One wrong step and the river took you.

He'd been halfway through rigging a harness on a kid no older than ten when the radio in his ear had crackled.

"Wall breach, south side," someone had shouted over the roar. "We've got a slip—Hart, we need—"

The connection had shrieked, then gone dead.

For three minutes he'd lost contact with half his team. Three minutes when the only sounds in his headset were static and distant screaming. Three minutes in which his hands shook on the rope and he'd had to bite down on the rising panic that he'd left Callie for this—to fail someone else instead.

They'd got the team back. No fatalities. Two broken ribs, a dislocated shoulder, a near-drowning that turned into a bad story told later over warm beer. On paper, the op was a success.

He'd spent that night sitting outside the field tent, soaked to the bone, staring into jungle-dark, knuckles white on a mug of cold coffee, listening for a heartbeat that wasn't his. The fear that had crawled into his bones then had never really left.

Now, in Crimson Creek, with Callie sleeping ten metres away and a stalker promising the word MINE in angry ink, that fear took a different shape.

Back then, he'd been terrified of losing control of a scene. Of not having enough hands or enough rope.

Now, he was terrified of losing her again.

✦ ✦ ✦

A soft sound broke the loop—the rustle of a blanket, the faint thump of bare feet on the mezzanine floor.

"Jax?"

Her voice, sleepy-rough, slid around the corner. He turned.

Callie stood in the doorway of the cot room wrapped in a blanket, hair mussed, one cheek creased from the pillow. The sight of her here, alive and a little rumpled in his safe house, punched through him harder than anything a battlefield had managed.

"Sorry," she said. "Didn't mean to freak you out. You disappeared."

"Couldn't sleep," he said, setting the kettle back on its stand. "Didn't want to wake you."

She padded closer, blanket trailing like a cloak. The Mill's white light made her skin look pale, almost fragile, but the line of her jaw said otherwise. "You do realise standing in the dark watching screens is not the same as rest, right?"

"It's restful to me," he said.

"That's the saddest thing I've heard all week."

She stopped beside him, close enough that he could feel the warmth radiating from her. Her gaze flicked to the photo wall, caught on the old café picture, then shifted to his younger self in the Pegasus file.

"You kept that?" she asked, nodding at her photo.

He shrugged, suddenly aware of how it looked. "Didn't want to forget what I was fighting for."

"And him?" She tipped her chin at his own image. "That bloke looks like he thinks he knows everything."

"He knew nothing," Jax said. "Except how to leave."

She studied his face, the way his mouth tightened around the last word. "You were a good man then."

"I made a bad choice," he said. "That cancels out a lot of good."

"Does it?" she asked softly. "Or does it just mean you were a scared one?"

He met her eyes, surprised. In the dim light, they looked almost the same as the girl in the old photo, but there was a depth now that grief and survival had carved into her.

"You asked me once," she continued, "what I would've done if you'd stayed. If I'd forgiven you before you left."

"I remember."

"I don't know," she said simply. "Maybe I would've resented you for watching her die. Maybe we would've fallen apart anyway. Or maybe we would've been stronger. I can't pretend there's only one version of that story."

He swallowed. "You told me you'd never forgive me."

"I did." Her mouth twisted. "I was twenty-two and dramatic and terrified. I needed somewhere to put all that. You were convenient."

He huffed a humourless laugh. "Glad I could be of service."

She nudged his arm with her shoulder. "Did you think I meant it forever?"

"Yes," he said, before he could stop himself. "I did."

Silence stretched between them, filled with the hum of the generator and the distant rush of the river.

"I tried," she said after a moment, voice smaller. "I tried to forgive. Then I tried to forget. Then I came here and pretended neither of us existed. Turns out pretending is exhausting."

"I'm good at it," he said. "Doesn't make it smart."

Her gaze flicked to his wrapped forearm. "You still collecting scars to prove you're useful?"

"They're a side effect," he said. "Useful's overrated."

"That the soldier talking?"

"That's the idiot who left you," he replied. "The soldier has a clearer job description."

She shifted so she was leaning against the same stretch of bench, shoulder pressed to his. The contact was small but solid.

"Tell me something," she said. "If you had your time again—same day, same window, same stamped passport in your pocket—would you go?"

He thought about the hospice room. Ellen's thin smile. Callie's red-rimmed eyes. The weight of the Pegasus contract in his hand—numbers that promised security, a future, a house that wouldn't be repossessed.

"Yes," he said quietly. "But I would tell you exactly why. And then I would come back sooner. Or not go as long. Or... I don't know." He shook his head. "I'd do the same stupid thing with a little more honesty."

She considered that, eyes on the kettle as it began to tremble. "You know what I wish?"

"What?"

"I wish you'd stayed long enough to see that I survived the thing you were trying to protect me from."

"Losing her," he said.

"Losing her," she echoed. "You didn't have to save me from that. You just had to stand in it."

He closed his eyes briefly. The truth of it landed heavy and clean.

"I'm standing now," he said.

"I've noticed," she replied, a small smile ghosting her mouth. "You've done nothing but stand between me and danger since you rolled into town."

"It's what I'm good at."

"It's not all you're good at," she said quietly.

The kettle shrieked, startling them both. She laughed, the sound cutting through the heaviness.

"You and that thing," she said. "Always on the edge of boiling over."

"Pot, meet kettle," he said.

Her smile widened. "Fair."

He poured water, the steam clouding the window for a moment. Outside, the street cameras ticked through their loop, oblivious to the two figures in the pool of fluorescent light.

"Why are you really awake?" she asked, softer now. "And don't say 'habit.' I know you better than that."

He stared at the rising vapour, trying to find words that didn't sound like excuses.

"Because last time I left you," he said slowly, "you had to do all the hard parts alone. This time, if something happens, I want to be awake for it. I want to see it coming."

"You're not responsible for every bad thing that might happen to me," she said.

"I know," he said. "But I'm still going to try to stop them."

She watched him over the rim of her mug, something easing in her shoulders.

"Do you regret coming back?" she asked. "To Crimson Creek. To me."

He didn't hesitate. "Not one second. I regret every day I stayed away."

The honesty surprised him as much as it seemed to surprise her. She blinked once, twice, then set her mug down with care.

"Then maybe," she said, "we stop pretending this is just about a threat assessment and a bad man with a worse handwriting style."

He almost smiled. "What do we call it instead?"

"Bad timing," she said. "New chance."

The words settled between them like another promise, unspoken but real.

A soft buzz from the console broke the moment—Maya's overnight script pinging a motion blip on the far side of town. Jax glanced at the feed. Just a fox slipping between bins behind the bakery.

Still, he logged the time. Habit. Armour. Prayer.

Callie watched him finish the notation, then touched her fingers lightly to the back of his hand.

"Come back to bed," she said, the invitation simple, not loaded. "You're not a very good wall when you're running on fumes."

"You sleep," he said. "I'll be there in a bit."

She arched a brow. "You don't trust the fox?"

"I don't trust the quiet," he said.

She considered him for a long moment, then nodded. "Okay. But at some point, you're going to have to trust that I can stand too. Not just behind you. Beside."

He felt that like a shift in the building's foundations.

"I'm working on it," he said.

"Work faster," she replied, then turned, blanket swishing as she padded back to the cot room.

He watched until she was out of sight. Then he turned back to the monitors, to the café camera, to the empty bridge. The ghosts on the wire were still there—choices he'd made, people he'd left, storms he'd walked into.

But so was she.

He set a timer for an hour, forced himself to lie down on the narrow bunk in the storeroom, and closed his eyes. The Mill breathed around him—steel ribs creaking, generator heart steady. Somewhere beyond, a man who thought the word MINE was a claim was watching.

Jax let the darkness come, just long enough to gather strength.

This time, he promised himself, he wasn't running.

7

CHAPTER 7 - BURIED SECRETS

Crimson Creek, Queensland — The Pegasus Mill

Morning came pale and thin, light seeping through the boarded window like it was afraid to touch what the night had broken. The air still smelled of dust and rain, a mix that never quite settled. The generator hummed low, steady as a bruise.

Jax hadn't slept. Callie had, barely—an hour, maybe—curled on the cot with the blanket pulled up to her chin, pretending the scrape of metal outside was just the wind and not the echo of glass exploding inward.

Now she sat at the bench, hands wrapped around a mug of cold coffee, eyes fixed on the note that lay between them. The paper had dried overnight, crimson ink bleeding into the fibres. The word *MINE* had spread like a wound.

Maya snapped photos of it from three angles—click, adjust, click—and slid the paper into an evidence sleeve. The plastic made a soft hiss as it sealed.

"Ink's alcohol-based," she said. "Marker, not paint. Could've been bought anywhere. No useful brand markers on the solvent content."

"Prints?" Logan asked from where he leaned against the steel door, arms folded. He looked like he'd been poured into his clothes and left to dry—creased, functional, awake.

"Maybe two partials that don't belong to either of you," Maya said. "I'll run them when I get back to the Switchyard board."

Jax stood by the window, jaw tight, hands braced on the sill. The plywood panel they'd thrown up after the brick hit was still rough-cut, edges splintered. The room around him carried the faint, angry smell of fresh sawdust.

"He's escalating," Jax said.

"He's desperate," Maya corrected. "He broke the rhythm. That means you're under his skin."

Callie let out a small, humourless laugh. "Good. Maybe he'll crawl out where I can see him."

"You'll get that chance," Logan said, voice gentler than his usual smart-arse. "We'll keep eyes on the café block. No more solo shifts. And I'll have Chase install a panic buzzer under your counter—links straight to us."

"I don't want my customers thinking they're walking into a war zone," Callie said, fingers tightening around the mug.

Logan tipped his head. "Then make the coffee good enough they won't notice. Fear tastes bitter. You'll fix that."

Maya closed her laptop with a soft click. "I'll run Pierce's name again. He's still the only connection from before Crimson Creek who fits the psychology."

At the sound of that name, Callie's shoulders stiffened. The tiny tremor went right through the mug.

"Evan's not here," she said. "He wouldn't risk it."

"Maybe not," Maya allowed. "But you've got history. And he's got the temperament. Possessive, controlling, curated public persona. He ticks the boxes."

"You don't know him," Callie said, staring at the note in the evidence sleeve.

"Don't need to," Maya replied. "The pattern speaks louder than charm."

Jax crossed the space and gently eased the mug from Callie's hands before she spilt it. Up close, he could see the pale crescents her nails had left in her palms.

"You okay?" he asked quietly.

"Fine," she said automatically.

He lifted a brow. "Try again."

She swallowed, eyes still on the word bleeding through plastic. "If it's Evan... if it's really him, then this is my fault."

"The hell it is," Jax said.

"I brought it here," she insisted, voice thin. "I thought I was starting over, but maybe I just gave it a new address. New scenes for the same story."

"Callie," he said, soft and steady, "you don't get to blame yourself for someone else's sickness. You didn't invite it. You survived it."

She blinked hard, but the tears didn't fall. "Feels like I dragged it along anyway."

"You left," he said. "That's the opposite of dragging."

Across the room, Maya slung her laptop bag over her shoulder, tactful enough to give them space. "I'll send updates once the lab hits back." She nodded to Logan. "We'll be at the Switchyard. Call if you even think you see something move."

Logan pushed off the door, the steel frame creaking in faint protest. "I'll grab Chase and get your panic button installed. Red Wolf," he added, tipping an invisible hat Callie-wards, "we're not going anywhere."

When they were gone, silence folded over the Mill again. Not empty—just thick. The generator hummed, a low, stubborn heartbeat against the metal ribs of the building.

Callie traced the rim of the mug with one finger, following the chipped porcelain, anchoring herself on imperfections.

"Maya's wrong about one thing," she said at last.

"Only one?" Jax asked, trying for light.

"Evan doesn't lose control," she said. "He plans. He rehearses. He rehearsed everything." Her mouth twisted. "He used to correct my facial expressions before we walked into a meeting."

"Then this wasn't him," Jax said, nodding at the evidence sleeve. "The guy who threw that brick—he's running on adrenaline. Too messy for a strategist. That word's a tantrum, not a manifesto."

"So someone else," she murmured. "Someone here. Someone who learned my flinch second-hand."

He nodded once. "We're narrowing the field."

49

Outside, the river moved slow and brown beneath the bridge, carrying yesterday's storm south. Through a gap at the edge of the boarded window, a thin strip of light picked out dust motes turning in the air. The quiet had that tight, stretched quality that always came before something snapped.

Callie pushed back from the bench, chair legs grating on the concrete. "I can't sit here all day. The café needs opening."

He frowned. "You really think that's smart?"

"No," she said. "But it's necessary."

He waited.

"If I hide, he wins," she said. "If I go back to normal, maybe he shows his hand. Besides, someone's got to serve Maya's caffeine addiction or she'll arrest the whole town."

He wanted to argue. He also knew she was right.

"Okay," he said. "But I'll be nearby."

"Of course you will," she said. "You're practically furniture now."

He almost smiled. "Rude."

They left the Mill together. Sunlight caught the moisture on the cobbles outside, turning it to glitter. The town was waking—delivery vans grumbling, a kid on a bike weaving between puddles, the butcher hosing down the footpath while his radio crackled old country songs. From the outside, Crimson Creek looked like any other morning.

Callie unlocked the café door. The little bell gave its bright, false cheer. Inside, everything smelled of cinnamon and coffee grounds, familiar enough to steady her heartbeat. She let the scent wash over her like a story she'd written herself.

She turned the sign to OPEN, flipped the switch on the espresso machine, and told herself the worst was over.

It wasn't.

Across the street, parked in the slant of shade under a gum tree, a dark sedan idled just long enough. The driver finished watching her before pulling away.

Jax watched it go from his reflection in the window glass. The back of his neck prickled.

"See something?" Callie asked.

"Maybe," he said. "Maybe not. Either way, we're not alone."

She nodded, fingers tightening around the filter handle. "We never were."

Crimson Creek — Late Morning, Red Wolf Books & Brew

The morning trade was kind. Regulars rolled in like punctuation marks—Mr DiAngelo the greengrocer first, still smelling of coriander and wet crates; then the postie, shaking rain off his cap; then two teachers with the brittle laughter of people already done with the day by ten a.m.

Callie held the rhythm and let it hold her back. Grind. Tamp. Pull. Smile. The machine settled into its familiar song; the milk jug hissed; the air warmed with cinnamon and steamed milk. For ten-minute stretches, life almost remembered how to be normal.

Jax took a table by the window, laptop open, one ear tuned to comms, the other to the street. From the outside he looked like a man doing emails. He was not a man doing emails.

At ten to ten, the bell chimed and a woman stepped in who didn't belong to any of Callie's categories.

Dark denim jacket. Boots that had seen real rain and real dirt. Hair twisted into a loose knot like it lived in a helmet half the time. She carried a recorder the size of a wallet and a tote that read: **LISTEN HARDER**.

"Hey," the woman said, voice comfortable, not chirpy. "You must be Callie. I'm Mara Bell."

She eased the recorder out just enough to show it, then set it on the counter face-down.

"Not recording unless you say so."

"Okay," Callie said carefully. "Can I get you something?"

"Flat white, thanks." Mara slid a business card across the counter—

Mara Bell – Cold Case // Warm Hands (Podcast).

The logo was a pair of headphones wrapped around a coffee cup.

"I'm doing a series on stalking cases that slipped through the gaps," she said. "Heard Crimson Creek had a story breathing heavier than most."

"We serve coffee," Callie said. "No gaps."

Mara smiled, accepting the parry. "Sure. But we both know someone's been writing you notes." Her eyes flicked to the windows, then to Jax. "And you've got a very polite shadow."

"Pegasus Security Services," Jax said, not looking up from the laptop.

Mara's brows lifted half a centimetre. "Right. Good neighbours."

She took her coffee when Callie slid it across, sipped, nodded once in professional approval. "That's beautiful. Mind if I ask some off-the-record questions? I'm not here to make a mess. Stalking thrives in silence. People need language."

Callie hesitated. She could feel Jax watching without watching, his attention a steady weight in the room.

"We're open," she said. "You can ask. Just... be gentle."

"I'm very good at gentle," Mara said. She tucked the recorder back into her tote, then pulled out a small envelope and lowered her voice. "Before we do that, I need to show you something. And—heads up—it'll sting."

She laid a photo on the counter between them.

Grainy. Daylight. City background. A man in a crisp shirt outside a glass-fronted office building—tidy beard, expensive watch, one hand curled possessively on a young woman's shoulder as she tried to step away. The woman was Callie, hair shorter, two years younger, smile stretched into politeness that didn't reach her eyes.

Air left the room for a second. The grinder's hum blurred. Callie had the visceral sensation of falling backwards into a year she'd boarded up and labelled Do Not Enter.

"Where did you get that?" she whispered.

"Friend at a paper in the city owes me a favour," Mara said evenly. "I asked for crowd shots outside Trident Media, six months before you left. He's in half a dozen. So are you."

Jax stood, the chair legs whispering across the floor. He reached the counter without looking like he'd rushed, but every muscle in his jaw said otherwise.

"What's your angle, Bell?" he asked.

"Context," Mara said. "This is Evan Pierce, yes?"

Callie's throat worked. "Yes."

"Ex-boss who liked boundaries as concepts, not practices," Mara continued. "Promoted you, praised you, forgot where he ended and you began?"

"Something like that," Callie said, forcing the words out.

"Do you have a current AVO?" Mara asked.

Callie shook her head. "I left. I blocked him. He sent three emails I didn't answer. It... tapered."

"Predators prefer perseverance to tapering," Mara said, but her tone stayed soft, not superior. "Did he ever show up in Crimson Creek?"

"No," Callie said immediately. Then, less sure, "Not that I've seen."

Mara slid the photo back into the envelope. "I'm not saying he's your current problem. You may have another admirer closer to home. But profiles echo. If he taught you fear, someone else learned your flinch."

Jax's voice sanded flatter. "What do you want from us?"

"To help you name it," Mara said. "And to keep him from hiding inside the story he's writing. Stalkers love their own narratives. I like to interrupt."

Callie studied her. "And if interrupting puts me in more danger?"

"Then I back off," Mara said instantly. "No interview goes out without your consent. No detail that maps to your door. I'm not here to make a meal of your life. I'm here because I've seen what happens when women keep serving coffee and pretending the notes aren't real."

"The notes are very real," Callie said quietly.

"Then we treat them like evidence," Mara replied. "And we treat you like a person, not a plot."

The bell chimed; a couple wandered in, cheeks pink from the chill outside. Callie poured, smiled, made change with hands that trembled once and then steadied. When the rush passed, she returned to Mara, who was now sketching a rough map of the block on a napkin—angles of sight, alley, planter box.

"You knew about the planter," Jax said.

Mara's mouth quirked. "Your boy Chase posted a blurred lens photo last year—different case, different town. I recognised the make. People in my line of work trade notes. I don't go where I'm not invited," she added, glancing at Callie. "This is me knocking."

Callie exhaled, tension thinning just enough to let air in. "You can ask," she said. "Not with the recorder. Not yet."

"'Not yet' is a good word," Mara said. "It means you decide when."

She slid another photo across—this one a group shot in a city bar. Callie on the edge of the frame, Evan just behind her with an arm not quite touching, posture tilted toward possession.

"Ever see him borrow power from other people's bodies?" Mara asked.

Callie's mouth went dry. "All the time."

"People like that leave fingerprints on rooms," Mara said. "This town will have noticed if he walked its streets. I'll ask quiet."

"You go through me," Jax said.

"I can live with that," Mara replied. She finished her coffee, set the cup down precisely, and met Callie's eyes. "My number's on the card. If you decide to talk, I'll listen on your terms."

Callie nodded. "Thanks."

Mara's smile tilted. "And for what it's worth? You look like someone who survived. That's a better story than whatever he's trying to write."

When she left, the bell chimed like punctuation at the end of a hard sentence. The café filled back around the space she'd created; people reclaimed the air with small talk and spoons on ceramic.

Jax moved to the far end of the counter with her, out of earshot. "You okay?"

Callie folded Mara's card once, twice, until it was smaller than her palm. "She's not wrong."

"About which part?" he asked.

"All of it," Callie said. She steadied herself on the stainless steel edge. "If Evan isn't the hand on the brick, he's still the ghost in the room. And if someone else is copying his script..."

"Then we burn the script," Jax said. "And we teach him fear isn't a leash."

The bell chimed again. A familiar silhouette filled the doorway—Noah Briggs. Clean T-shirt, toolbox in one hand, the easy smile of a man who believes in his own helpfulness.

"Morning, Cal," he said. "Heard about the window. Brought sealant for that back-door gap. Won't take a second."

Jax stepped into his line of sight, polite, immovable. "We're good, Noah. Professional's handling it."

Noah paused, measuring the temperature. His smile held, but his eyes cooled half a degree. "Sure," he said. "Just thought I'd offer."

"Appreciate it," Callie said. "Another time."

He nodded, tapped the doorframe with two fingers in a gesture that pretended to be nothing, and left. The bell chimed once—a bright sound that, today, felt like teeth.

Callie watched him cross to his ute and sit for a long beat before pulling away. She didn't exhale until the taillights disappeared.

"Stay visible," Jax said quietly.

"I plan to."

The morning wore on. Between the ten-thirty rush and the quiet that followed, Callie's phone buzzed twice with unknown numbers and once with a message from a blocked contact. She didn't open it.

At eleven-fifteen, she wiped the counter and reached for her mobile again.

"I'm going to run next door and ask Mrs Keegan about that sedan," she said. "She notices everything. She probably knows who bought the number plates in 1998."

"I'll go," Jax said.

"She'll talk to me," Callie replied, tucking the phone into her apron. "Two minutes."

He frowned. "Make it one."

She grinned like she meant to obey, grabbed the receipt pad, and ducked out into the bright. The bell chimed. The door swung back on its hinges and came to rest half-open.

A minute later, the phone on the counter buzzed. Then again.

The screen lit with a text she'd begun, unsent, the cursor blinking at the end of four words:

I think I know—

✦ ✦ ✦

Crimson Creek — 11:22 a.m.

The bell over the café door had stopped swinging. The coffee machine hissed once, then settled into a low idle. Jax looked up from the back table and knew—before he reached the counter—that something was wrong.

Callie's phone lay there, screen glowing. The draft message stared up at him:

I think I know—

He whispered her name once. "Callie?"

No answer.

The street outside shimmered with heat, bright and ordinary. The butcher hosed down the pavement two doors up. A delivery van rumbled past. A cyclist waved at nobody in particular.

Nothing looked like danger—until you noticed the quiet.

He hit the comm in his ear. "Pegasus One to base. Hart's gone."

Logan's voice snapped back, sharper than usual. "Repeat?"

"She's missing," Jax said, already moving around the counter and out the door. "Left her phone. Last text: *I think I know—*"

"Lock down the block," Logan said. "I'm two minutes out."

Maya cut in, breathless through static. "Trace her device."

"Already in my hand," Jax said, scanning the street. No sign of her. No Keegan on the stoop. No Callie silhouette anywhere. "GPS pings right here. She didn't take it."

"Try her smartwatch," Maya said. "If she's wearing it, I can triangulate."

Jax sprinted to the four-wheel drive, engine turning before the door shut. His heart was a cold, hard thing in his chest.

"Do it," he said.

There was a pause. Keys clacked faintly over the line. Maya's voice came back clipped, all business.

"Signal's moving," she said. "South-west. Rail-yard perimeter. Four blocks."

Jax's grip tightened on the wheel. "Copy."

He hit the siren toggle—one short burst, just enough to scatter pigeons and pedestrians—then killed it. He didn't want noise. He wanted speed.

Crimson Creek blurred past in red brick and sunlight. The old mills rose ahead like rusted sentries, their faded lettering spelling out the bones of a town that once built engines and now built nothing but memory. The closer he got, the quieter it became.

Maya's voice rode in his ear, steady and low. "Logan's two blocks behind you. Chase is tracing CCTV. No vehicles leaving the yard in the last five minutes. No registered movement on the western exit."

Jax swung the car into the gravel lot and killed the engine. Heat hit him like a wall the moment he stepped out. The air smelled of oil, old rain, and rust.

"Visual?" Logan asked.

"Yard looks empty," Jax murmured. "Smartwatch says she's inside the perimeter. Distance... fifty metres, bearing north-east."

He moved fast but quiet, gun drawn low, breath measured. The main warehouse loomed ahead—sheet-metal walls, paint flaking, one roller door half-open like a lazy mouth. Her bag sat near the entrance, strap torn.

His stomach turned to stone.

"Logan, I've got eyes on her pack," he said. "Going in."

Inside, light filtered through broken windows in long, cathedral stripes. Dust hung in the air like smoke. The echo of his footsteps came back at him off concrete and steel.

For a moment there was only silence.

Then—

"Jax?"

Her voice. Small, hoarse, but real. It slid under his ribs like a blade and a blessing.

"Callie?" he called back, softer than he felt.

He followed the sound to the far end of the hall. She sat against the wall, wrists tied in front of her with thinner rope than he'd expected, the knots loose, like whoever tied them hadn't decided whether to commit. A cut marked her cheek where glass or concrete had kissed her. Her breathing was too fast, but steady.

He dropped to his knees beside her, muzzle dropping, training abandoning everything but her. He checked pulse, pupils, the line of her throat.

"You hurt anywhere else?" he asked.

She shook her head, eyes filling. "He was here."

"Who?" he asked.

Her throat worked. "I didn't see his face. He came from behind. Smelt like... turps and sweat." Her hands shook against the rope. "He said, *You don't look at me anymore.* Like I owed him my eyes." Her breath hitched. "Then the door slammed and I heard tyres."

Jax's gaze slid past her to the wall behind.

Words had been carved deep into the sheet metal. Letters rough and deliberate:

SHE'S MINE.

Fresh cuts. Paint still curling along the grooves.

He keyed his mic with his free hand. "Pegasus, confirm location. I've got her. Warehouse Four, northern wall. He's gone."

Logan's reply came hard, boots already pounding through the static. "We're on you. Sit tight. Yard's boxed."

Jax holstered his weapon, fished his pocketknife out and slid the blade under the rope. The fibres gave with a reluctant snap. He pulled her gently forward, feeling the tremor in her muscles like an echo of his own.

Her heartbeat thundered against his shoulder when he drew her in. Too fast. Too alive.

"It's okay," he said, one hand between her shoulder blades. "You're okay. I've got you."

She shook her head against him. "He's not done," she murmured into his shirt.

He looked over her shoulder at the words on the wall. They looked back at him, raw and rude and wrong.

"I know," he said quietly. "But he just told us exactly what he is."

Footsteps pounded closer. Logan's silhouette filled the doorway a moment later, gun high, eyes scanning before he let them soften slightly at the sight of her upright.

"Bloody hell, Red Wolf," he said, breathless. "You trying to give us all heart attacks?"

She let out a broken laugh that wasn't really a laugh at all.

Behind Logan, sirens began to echo—one, then another—the town waking late to its own danger. Dust lifted from the floor in their wake, swirling like smoke through the shafts of light.

Jax helped Callie stand, arm firm around her waist. Her knees wobbled once, then locked.

"Can you walk?" he asked.

"Yeah," she said. Her voice shook, but it carried. "I'm not staying in here a second longer."

He nodded. "Good."

As they turned for the door, the words on the wall caught the light—

SHE'S MINE glowing like a warning no one could unsee.

Callie felt them at her back like eyes.

"He's wrong," she said under her breath.

"What?" Jax asked.

She straightened, every small, stubborn part of her rising at once.

"I don't belong to anyone," she said.

And she walked out of Warehouse Four with her head high, leaving the carved words to rust.

8

CHAPTER 8 — ONE LAST STAND

Crimson Creek, Queensland — Early Evening

They rolled back into the Pegasus Mill with the sun dragging a red edge along the roofline, the kind of light that made everything look dipped in rust. The building took them in the way it always did—steel ribs creaking, generator humming low, the faint oil-and-rain smell wrapped around the bones of the place like memory.

Logan was waiting at the side door, jaw set, shirt damp at the collar from running the yard. "You're late," he said, then softer when he clocked Callie's taped cheek, "You're okay."

"She is," Jax said. "Warehouse Four. He staged it. Rope was loose."

"Showed his hand to prove he has hands," Logan muttered. "Theatre kid with a knife."

Inside, the Mill buzzed like a quiet war room. Maya sat at the workstation, three monitors blooming with feeds—council cameras, road exits, lifeless alleyways. Her eyes never stopped moving.

"Pulled number plates in a five-block radius around the yard," she said. "Three I can vouch for. One's a rental on a day rate, cash deposit, prepaid card. No ID worth the pixels it's printed on."

Chase was half on the mezzanine, half in a nest of cable, coax looped around his shoulders like vines. "Mill's buttoned. You've got a ten-metre bubble. If he sneezes in it, I'll say bless you."

Callie stepped over the threshold and the door thunked shut behind her, a solid, hollow sound that felt like punctuation at the end of a nightmare sentence. Her skin still held the chill of the warehouse; the warmth of the Mill climbed slowly up her arms.

"He said I don't look at him anymore," she said quietly. "Like I owed him my eyes."

The room stilled.

"Good," Logan said. "Means he's noticed what we're taking back."

Jax pressed a stainless cup of water into her hand. "Drink."

She did. The metallic tang grounded her. Her gaze drifted to the screens—streets, corners, reflections in glass. So many places a person could hide. So many angles where she'd never thought to look.

Maya spun her chair, posture coiled but voice careful. "We need to redraw the board. He's moving faster now. That's good and bad."

"Bad first," Logan said.

"Fewer pauses, shorter windows, higher risk," Maya replied. "Good second—more opportunities for screw-ups. And men like this always screw up when they think they're close."

"Then we give him something to think he's close to," Logan said. "Controlled. Contained. Unforgiving."

Callie wrapped both hands around the cup, knuckles pale. "And I get a say in what that looks like this time."

All three Pegasus faces turned to her. Jax's first answer was in his eyes—fear, pride, something rawer—before his voice caught up.

"You get more than a say," he said. "You get veto power."

She nodded once, as if confirming something with herself. "Then here's my condition. We stop letting him write the scenes. We show him a version of me he can't script—public, loud, not alone. If he's been studying my habits, we give him a new one to choke on."

Logan's mouth tipped. "Look at you, running a production meeting."

"You thought I opened a café without knowing how to run a floor?" she shot back.

"Wouldn't dream of it," he said, grin brief and real.

Maya turned back to the main monitor. "The Switchyard's too noisy. Too many exits, too many bodies. The café's too familiar—he's mapped every inch. Community hall by the river has the best geometry. Two doors, both lockable. Windows high, angles clean."

"Charity pop-up," Callie said, already seeing it. "Books, coffee, music. We advertise. He's been watching my socials. He'll see it."

"Not tonight," Jax said immediately. "We're not sprinting to his timetable."

"No," she agreed. "Tonight, I just need one chapter that isn't about him at all."

Logan raised a brow. "What are you thinking?"

She looked at Jax. The decision in her eyes was quiet and absolute. "You said there's a cabin out near the dam."

He held her gaze. "Rescue training site. One road in. Good locks. Better sightlines."

"Take me there," she said. "Just for a night. I can't fall asleep staring at the word MINE on a wall and wake up sane."

Logan let out a low whistle. "Now that is a good call. I'll sit the café, charm the locals, loiter like a hungover saint. Maybe I'll sell some of your muffins as hazard pay."

"Don't get arrested," Maya said dryly.

"Please," Logan sniffed. "If anyone's locking me up, it's for my personality, not my methods."

Chase bounded down from the mezzanine, cable looped in precise circles. "Give me an hour to lace your route," he said. "I'll seed trackers along the dam road. If anyone hugs your bumper, I'll see what brand of aftershave he wears."

He dug in the Pelican and held out a tiny black rectangle to Callie. "Pocket alarm. One press brings Pegasus. The other brings the cops. Hold for three seconds and it screams loud enough to make angels flinch."

She closed her fingers around it. The shape sat snug in her palm, small but solid. "Thank you."

Maya crossed the room and squeezed Callie's forearm, a rare unarmoured touch. "You did nothing to deserve him," she said softly. "We'll make sure your bones know that, not just your head."

Callie swallowed hard. "I'm starting to believe you."

Maya stepped back to her screens; the armour slid back on with a quiet click.

Jax moved closer, voice pitched just for her. "You're sure about the cabin? It's quiet. No distractions. Just you, me, and a kettle that screams like it's being murdered."

"Perfect," she said. "I'm tired of being afraid in crowds. I'd like to try not being afraid somewhere still."

He nodded once. It felt like a vow. "Pack what you need. We'll leave at dusk."

Logan clapped Jax on the shoulder as he passed. "Take the long road—less chance of tails. And text me the second you see water. If you don't, I'm bringing half the bar and a disco ball."

"Spare us," Jax said.

Chase tossed him a roll of black tape. "For the dome light. Last thing we need is a two-person diorama at every red light."

Jax caught it. "Thoughtful."

The sky outside slid from rust to bruise as the afternoon tipped toward evening. The Mill hummed around them, cables, metal, quiet intent.

Jax led Callie to the back room where a steel cabinet had become a kind of emergency wardrobe. Inside: folded hoodies, sealed toothbrushes, socks, basics. The sight winded her a little—how many women had stood here before, needing a life in miniature until theirs was safe again.

"Take what fits," he said. "Pegasus hospitality's not glamorous, but it's clean."

She chose a soft grey jumper and thick socks, thumb brushing over the label on a tiny, unopened moisturiser. The sheer normality of it nearly undid her.

He pretended not to notice the wobble, turning away just enough to give her a moment. She didn't use it. She capped the feeling, tucked it neatly beside all the others she didn't have time to unpack, and turned back to him.

"What about you?" she asked. "You planning to pack anything besides a knife and a bad plan?"

"Rude," he said. "I always bring at least two bad plans."

Her laugh was small but real. "Add a blanket. I get cold."

"You'll have one," he said. His eyes held hers. "You'll have me."

The words hung there, not a claim, just an offering. She let them settle, then nodded once, accepting.

"Then let's go," she said. "Before I talk myself out of being brave."

They reconvened at the side door as the horizon bled out to purple. Logan handed Callie a paper bag that smelled suspiciously like comfort.

"Crew chow," he announced. "Sandwiches, stew, two apples, and something mysterious in foil that Chase swears is edible."

"Best bet is don't look at it in direct light," Chase advised from the mezzanine.

Maya leaned on the rail above them. "I'll geofence the cabin. You cross that line, I know it. Anything else crosses, I know that too."

Chase gave a thumbs-up. "Dash cam's live, rear cam's hot, and the dome light now believes in the dark. You're a moving CCTV lesson."

"Romantic," Callie said.

"You should see my Valentine's setups," he shot back.

The side door opened on cool, iron-scented air. The Mill made a low, metal sound as they stepped out—a noise that somehow managed to say *go* and *come back* at the same time.

Logan locked the bar with a firm twist. "One last stand," he said to no one in particular, then louder, "Clean road. No surprises. Let's keep it that way."

The ute's engine caught on the first turn. Jax killed the interior light and waited until his eyes adjusted before pulling out. Callie settled into the passenger seat, buckled in, one palm pressed flat to her thigh until the muscle stopped trying to shake.

The Mill shrank in the side mirror—steel ribs, warm squares of light, a fortress built out of stubbornness and code.

"Ready?" Jax asked.

She looked at the road, at his hands on the wheel, at the way the dark opened in front of them and decided yes. "Ready."

Crimson Creek slid by in fragments—shops, the bridge, the painted railings, the river holding the last of the sky. With every kilometre the town loosened its hold and the hinterland took over, dark gums rising like silhouettes of old giants.

They drove without music, tyres singing their low, steady note. Every few minutes Jax's phone buzzed softly—Maya's check-ins, a digital heartbeat: **Clear. Clear. Still clear.**

Callie leaned her head against the window and watched the lights disappear behind a low curve in the road. She didn't look at her phone. She looked at the dark ahead and the man beside her and tried on the idea that somewhere out there, the world might have a place where nothing bad had ever happened.

"Tell me something ordinary," she said at last.

He thought for a moment. "The cabin's got two mugs that don't match, and a kettle that squeals like it's proud of itself every time it boils."

She smiled into the glass. "That'll do."

Crimson Creek Hinterland — Nightfall

The last servo in town shrank in the rear mirror, its neon sighing itself into distance. After that, the road narrowed, shoulders rough with gravel and grass, gums leaning in close enough for branches to scrape the ute's roof.

The headlights carved twin tunnels through the dark. Beyond their reach, the world was nothing but tree trunks and the rumour of more sky.

"Lots of stars out here," Callie said.

"Wait till the lake," Jax said. "No streetlights. Whole sky twice."

"Reflection," she murmured. "You always liked that word. Said it sounded alive."

"It is," he replied. "You just have to look long enough."

The bitumen gave way to dirt. The ute bumped along the rutted track, lantana brushing its flanks. The air tasted different out here—damp earth, eucalyptus, the first hint of water.

"You okay?" he asked quietly.

She checked in with herself. "I'm... less not-okay than I've been in a while."

"I'll take that," he said.

The trees thinned without warning, and the lake appeared—dark and glass-smooth, cradling the sky in its basin. The cabin stood near the waterline, weatherboard and corrugated iron, porch light off, chimney leaning a fraction left like it had been through a few more summers than it intended.

The ute rolled to a stop beneath a scribbly ironbark. Jax killed the engine. The silence that followed felt thick, like the world had been holding its breath waiting for them to arrive.

"This is it?" Callie asked.

"This is it," he said.

They sat for one shared heartbeat, then he stepped out and came around to her door. Gravel crunched under his boots. The air was cool enough to raise goosebumps.

When she climbed down, the night wrapped around her in one piece—no alleyways, no streetlights, no mirrors pretending to be safe. Just water. Trees. Sky.

She filled her lungs slowly. "It smells like pine and rain."

"Wait till morning. It'll smell like smoke and bad coffee."

She smiled. "Sold."

Inside, the cabin smelled of cedar, dust, and old storms. Jax flicked the breaker and a single bulb over the kitchen table sputtered to life, turning the small space gold.

Two rooms. Stone fireplace. Narrow kitchenette with mismatched crockery. A folded blanket on the back of a sagging couch. A kettle that squealed as soon as he set it on the gas.

"Welcome to luxury accommodation," he said.

She turned in a slow circle. "You undersold the view."

He checked the doors, the latches, the windows with quiet, practised movements—testing, tightening, making the place answer to him. When he was done, something in his shoulders eased a fraction.

Callie went to the window. The lake outside held a perfect copy of the sky—stars scattered, a thin coin of a moon, a smudge of cloud where the storm had wandered away. In the glass she saw her reflection and his behind her, taller, watchful.

"It's strange," she said. "Everything's still. Like the world's holding its breath."

"Maybe it's waiting for you to exhale," he said.

She looked back at him, barefoot now, sleeves pushed up, firelight already imagining itself on his face. "You really think we can trap him?"

"I think we can make him pick where to fall apart," Jax said. "And be waiting to catch the pieces."

"And the part where I get to live after?"

He held her eyes. "That's the only part that matters."

The kettle chose that moment to scream. They both jumped, then laughed, the sound bouncing off the timber and making the place feel less like a hideout and more like a holiday house someone forgot to sell.

They took their tea to the front porch. The boards creaked under their weight, but nothing complained. The night was full of soft noises—frogs singing down near the reeds, a fish breaking the surface with a small splash, the wind worrying the tops of the gums.

"You know," she said, cupping her mug, "if you'd told me a week ago I'd be hiding out in a lakeside cabin with hired security, I'd have laughed."

"Hired security?" he said. "Ouch."

"Former soldier, current knight in flannel," she corrected. "Happy?"

"Getting there."

They sat without filling the air. The quiet here wasn't empty. It was full of everything that hadn't been said when life was louder.

"Storm's building out past the range," he said after a while, watching distant flashes behind the hills. "Might get rain later."

"Good," she said. "Mum always said storms wash bad days clean."

"Smart woman."

"She was," Callie agreed softly. "She used to say love isn't what you say when everything's perfect. It's what you do when it's falling apart."

He turned his mug in his hands. "What do you think she'd say about all this?"

"She'd tell you to stop running away from the people you love," Callie said. "And she'd tell me I'm allowed to stop apologising for him."

He swallowed. "Sounds about right."

They watched the lake and the sky for a long time, breaths gradually syncing with the water's slow rhythm.

"Ready to go in?" he asked.

"Just one more minute," she said. "I want to remember what stillness feels like."

So they gave her that.

Lakeside Cabin — After Midnight

The storm arrived like every Queensland storm—polite at first, then everywhere. Rain tapped the tin roof, tested it, then settled into a steady drumming that won against the frogs and the fire's crackle.

Inside, the cabin glowed. The fire Jax had coaxed to life filled the hearth, flames licking at old stone, light flickering over the table, the kettle, the faded curtains. Shadows jumped gently on the walls like memories they could almost name.

Callie sat cross-legged on the rug, hair loose, Jax's flannel shirt hanging off one shoulder. The colour had come back to her face, the fine strain at the corners of her mouth softened by heat and exhaustion.

Jax leaned against the wall beside the small window, curtain pulled back a handspan. Habit. One eye on the dark. One ear tuned to the rhythm of the rain.

"You do that a lot," she said, voice quiet.

"Do what?"

"Look at the dark like it owes you an explanation."

"Old habit," he said. "The dark usually does."

He pushed off the wall and joined her by the fire. The warmth soaked into his bones; the day finally started to leave his muscles.

"How long have you been doing this?" she asked. "Carrying the wall around with you."

"Since the first time it worked," he said. "After that it stops feeling like a choice."

They sat side by side, legs stretched towards the flames. The silence between them wasn't awkward. It was a place to rest.

"My mum was right about the storms," Callie said at last. "When I was little, she'd sit me at the window and say, 'Listen. That's the sky shaking out its pockets. Everything bad it picked up has to go somewhere.'"

"Where did you think it went?" he asked.

She smiled faintly. "Into the river. Into the sea. Somewhere big enough to hold it."

Another crack of thunder rolled over the hills. The cabin shivered; the fire snapped and then settled.

"She'd have liked you," Callie said.

"I'm not sure that's true," he replied.

"She would," Callie insisted. "She had a soft spot for broken things that still did their job."

He huffed a laugh. "Flattering."

"She'd also tell you to stop trying to protect everyone by disappearing."

He went quiet.

"When you left," she went on, voice careful, "I thought that was the lesson. That love means leaving before you do more damage. That you apologise by staying away."

"I was a coward," he said. No deflection. No pretty words. "I told myself it was duty. I chose the job because I was scared if I chose you, I'd fail you when it mattered. Turned out I did both anyway."

She stared into the fire, eyes glossy. "You weren't the only one who made that choice. I pushed you away when I needed you most. I thought if I hurt enough, I'd dodge the next hurt. That's not how it works."

He turned his hand palm-up on the rug between them, not quite touching hers. "I'm here now."

She looked at his hand, then at his face.

"Is that going to keep meaning something," she asked softly, "when we're not in the same room as a crime scene?"

"Yes," he said. "If you let it."

Lightning flashed, white and clean. For a heartbeat they saw each other

69

lit starkly—every line of fatigue, every old grief, every new fault. When the light went, they were still there.

She slid her hand into his.

It wasn't dramatic. Their fingers just… fit. Warm. Solid. Real.

They sat like that, watching the fire settle into coals, listening to the storm move along the valley, fingers laced.

"You don't have to keep pretending you're made of armour," she said after a while.

"And you don't have to pretend you're fine," he said.

"I'm terrified," she admitted. "But not of him. Not in the same way."

"What, then?"

"Of losing this before we even find out what it is."

He didn't inch closer, but everything in him leaned. "Then we don't," he said. "We don't let fear write this one."

"You can't control everything," she said.

He smiled, crooked. "You'd be amazed how many things I can make very uncomfortable."

She laughed, and the sound was bright enough to make the rain feel friendly.

They stayed there until the fire sank into embers and the storm softened to a steady patter.

"We should sleep," she said softly. "Before I start saying things I can't walk back."

"You already did," he replied. "So did I."

"True," she said. "So we sleep anyway."

He shifted as if to stand. "You take the bed. I'll take the floor."

"You'll wake up with half a spine," she said. "Not happening. There's room. One side each. We've survived worse proximity."

He hesitated, courtesy and desire tangling. "You sure?"

"I'm tired of being alone in rooms," she said simply. "Stay."

The word threaded through him like light through smoke.

"Okay," he said.

The bed was small, but they arranged themselves back-to-back, a careful handspan of mattress between them. The rain drummed. The lake breathed. The cabin creaked like it was telling its own old stories.

At some point, between one thunder roll and the next, she shifted in her sleep. So did he. The distance disappeared. Her hand found his. His fingers closed around hers.

No words.

Just the steady rhythm of two people who had spent a long time holding their breath, finally remembering how to let it go.

Sometime after three, a soft chime cut through the hush. Jax surfaced from sleep fast, years of training snapping him upright before his brain caught up.

The Pegasus tablet on the nightstand glowed. An alert flashed:

DOORBELL CAM — RED WOLF BOOKS — MOTION DETECTED.

He slid free without waking her and tapped the feed.

The café door filled the frame. Early-morning dark. Rain-shiny street. A figure on the step, close enough to the camera that his face warped slightly with the fisheye.

Noah Briggs.

Hair damp. Polite smile. A small white box in his hand.

Jax turned the volume up a fraction.

"Missed you, Cal," Noah's voice murmured, distorted but clear enough. "You shouldn't hide."

He reached out and stroked the door frame, fingers lingering exactly where Callie's hand always rested when she locked up. Then he stepped back into the rain and vanished out of frame.

The feed timed out. The alert winked away.

Jax stared at the darkened screen, jaw clenched hard enough to ache. The urge to move—to drive, to confront, to drag the man out of his own bones— burned hot and useless.

He turned his head.

Callie was still asleep, face turned toward the fire's dying glow, features soft in a way he hadn't seen in months. The cut on her cheek looked smaller. The lines at the corners of her mouth had smoothed.

"Not tonight," he whispered to the empty room. "You don't get to find her tonight."

He put the tablet face down, lay back on the bed, and let her hand find his again in the dark.

Outside, the last of the storm passed over the lake, leaving the water slick and new.

Inside, the cabin listened.

Dawn, when it came, would bring decisions, traps, and plans. But for the few hours left between lightning and first light, Crimson Creek could wait.

For once, Callie Hart slept.

And Jax, for the first time in longer than he cared to count, slept beside her.

9

CHAPTER 9 — MORNING ON STILL WATER

The storm drained itself by dawn.

A thin mist drifted low across the lake, turning the world into soft watercolour: pale silver sky, blurred gum silhouettes, a shoreline that looked dreamt into place. The air smelled rinsed—cedar, smoke, and the faint sweetness of wet earth.

Jax was already up.

Bare feet on cold timber. One hand wrapped around a mug whose steam had long surrendered. His eyes tracked the lake, watching light crawl across its surface. Storms didn't wash danger away, he knew. They just rearranged it.

Behind him, the bedroom breathed—blankets shifting, a small exhale, the quiet sound of someone waking without fear for the first time in too long.

Callie stepped into the doorway wearing his flannel shirt, sleeves bunched at her wrists. Her hair was loose, damp at the ends. In the soft lake light, she looked younger—not in years but in burden.

"How long have you been up?" she murmured.

"Long enough to convince the kettle we survived the night."

She smiled—an understated, real thing—and moved to stand beside him on the porch. Mist swirled around their ankles, the lake holding their reflections like truths waiting for their mouths.

"I don't remember the last time I slept through," she said. "No dreams. No glass shattering. Just dark."

"That's what safe feels like," he whispered.

"Feels foreign."

"It shouldn't."

Her gaze travelled over the water, calm and unbroken.

Then, softer: "You saw something last night, didn't you?"

He hesitated just long enough for her to know she was right.

"The café doorbell cam pinged at three," he said. "Someone came."

She stiffened. "Who?"

"Noah Briggs."

Her breath caught.

"He brought cookies," Jax added, jaw tightening. "Box in one hand. Smile in place."

Callie pressed her palms to the railing. "He lives four houses down. He used to fix things when I didn't ask. I thought he was just... kind."

"He isn't," Jax said carefully. "He's escalating. Watching. Testing the perimeter."

She drew a long, steadying breath. The fog curled around her like a shawl of cold light. "You think he's the one from the warehouse?"

"I think he wants you to think he could be," he said. "I think he wants control. Whether he's the brick-thrower or a shadow trying to look bigger— either way, he gets stopped."

Her hands tightened. "Good."

Jax turned to face her fully.

"We end this," he said. "On our terms."

Callie lifted her chin. "Then let's start. I'm done being afraid of men who whisper at doors."

He breathed once—slow, controlled—because her courage always hit him harder than any battlefield ever had.

She looked out over the shimmering lake.

"You think it'll rain again?"

"Probably," he said. "But not for a while."

"Good." She released a slow breath. "Let's pack before the sky changes its mind."

For the first time in a long time, her voice carried more resolve than dread.

For the first time, Jax believed they were no longer just surviving.

They were moving.

The drive back to Crimson Creek didn't feel like the drive out.

Morning painted the roads gold. Rain-washed bitumen gleamed. Birds moved through the trees in hectic arcs. The world—briefly, impossibly—felt clean.

Callie kept her hand loosely on her knee, no longer clawing at seams or counting heartbeats.

She didn't cling to silence this time.

She chose it.

Jax watched the road but kept half his focus centred on her breathing. Her softness. Her strength. The way her eyes scanned the horizon like she finally trusted she belonged in it.

By the time they reached town limits, the café row was waking—awnings rolling up, baristas yawning, shop windows steaming from the inside out.

Maya was waiting at the Mill entrance before they even parked.

"You look human," she said to Callie.

"That's a start," Callie replied.

Logan peeked from behind the door, a half-eaten muesli bar in hand. "She slept, didn't she?"

"She did," Jax said.

"Called it," Logan said smugly.

"Called what?" Callie asked.

"That you'd sleep once you got somewhere quiet."

Maya huffed. "You also said you'd eat only one muesli bar today, and we all know that was a lie."

Chase leaned over the mezzanine railing. "You made it back! Good! My panic levels were at a tasteful seven."

Jax exhaled the last of the night out of his lungs and switched gears.

"Okay," he said. "Status."

Maya hit a key. Screens lit with grids—street cams, exterior feeds, alleyway motion sensors.

"At dawn," she said, "we caught a sedan circling your street with the front plate obscured. Same model as the rail-yard vehicle. Driver kept his head down."

"Smart or scared," Logan said. "Both work for us."

Chase pointed at the monitors excitedly. "I've seeded trackers along your street and the back lane. He steps within fifty metres, I get six angles on him before he gets one on you."

Callie nodded. "Good. Because tomorrow... I reopen."

Jax tensed. "You sure?"

"Yes," she said, steady. "He wants the show. Let him watch the wrong one."

Maya smiled thinly. "Our girl's got teeth today."

"It's the sleep," Logan said. "Sleep makes rebels."

Callie moved closer to the board, eyes on her café windows, her street, her life.

"This time," she said, "I choose where the fear goes."

Jax came beside her. "And I choose where you stand."

Their shoulders brushed—not accidentally.

Late Afternoon — Pegasus Mill

Plans clicked into place with the easy precision of a team that had lived too long on alert.

Maya mapped entry points and exit angles.

Logan divided crowd flow and cover.

Chase ran the interior cameras like a man conducting symphonies no one else could hear.

Jax stood with Callie at the whiteboard calendar—now filled with tasks crossed out, arrows scribbled, new times added.

"You don't flinch when you see the café anymore," he murmured.

Her eyes stayed on the board. "Fear's a parasite. If you don't feed it, it dies."

He looked at her—not the words, but the truth behind them.

"You ready?"

She exhaled once.

"One last stand."

He nodded.

"Together."

"Always," she replied without thinking.

And they both stilled, because the word felt too natural to unpack.

The room quieted.

The plan was set.

The sun tilted its warm edge against Crimson Creek.

Tomorrow they would bait the hook.

Tomorrow they would close the trap.

Tomorrow they would force a man who thrived in shadows to step into the light.

But tonight—

tonight the world felt like it was shifting back toward her.

Jax saw it.

The others felt it.

The Mill hummed with the electricity of a story reaching for its climax.

Callie stood by the window, watching the town below.

Her reflection hovered faintly on the glass—stronger now, clearer now, someone coming home to herself.

"We end this," she whispered.

Behind her, Jax's voice came low and certain:

"We will."

And for the first time since the word MINE appeared on a wall of metal and fear—

Callie believed him.

10

CHAPTER 10 — THE BREATH BEFORE THE TRAP

Crimson Creek — The Day Before
Late Evening

The café smelled like cardamom and lemon zest.

Not fear.

Not brick dust.

Not the copper taint of the night the world cracked open.

Callie stood behind the counter, sleeves rolled, hair pinned back in a loose knot. The espresso machine hummed. The polished timber gleamed. The window glass shone like someone had gently asked it to forget it had ever been broken.

It felt like stepping back into herself — but taller.

Jax leaned in the doorway, arms folded. Watching. Always watching.

Not because she was fragile.

Because she mattered.

"You're sure?" he asked quietly.

"I am," she said.

He nodded once. He never pretended not to be afraid — but he also never pretended she wasn't strong enough to choose her path.

Chase whistled from the corner booth where he had disguised a field tablet under a battered café menu.

"This place has better surveillance than NASA," he said proudly.

Maya looked up from the counter she was wiping down. "NASA doesn't have to catch stalkers."

"True," Chase said. "Boring job."

Logan emerged from the storeroom carrying a box of paper cups. "All right. Positions?"

Maya pointed to the board taped to the fridge.

- **Callie:** *front-of-house, normal routine, no alterations.*
- **Jax:** *back corner table, clear sightlines, disguised as a tired tradie with a newspaper.*
- **Logan:** *alley door, rotating inside every ten minutes.*
- **Maya:** *control centre in the storeroom, screens live, phone lines open.*
- **Chase:** *undercover barista, pretending to understand coffee at a molecular level.*

Callie's mouth twitched.

"You can't steam milk."

Chase spread his hands. "But can he charm a Karen into believing the milk was steamed spiritually? Yes."

"Absolutely not," Maya muttered.

Callie turned to the window. The street outside was quiet — shops closing, last dog walkers heading home, the early dusk settling over the creek.

Tomorrow, the chalkboard would go back out.

Tomorrow, the door would unlock.

Tomorrow, she would step into the light on purpose.

Her chest rose and fell slowly.

"This feels like the last inhale before something big," she murmured.

"It is," Jax said behind her.

She didn't jump; she didn't startle; she didn't shrink.

Instead she turned and looked at him fully.

"What if tomorrow goes wrong?"

His gaze didn't waver.

"Then we make it right."

"And if it goes right?" she pressed.

"Then we end it."

The words settled like the first drop of rain before a storm — soft, but promising more.

The Mill — Later

They returned to Pegasus as night pulled itself over the town. The Mill's steel ribs glowed under the last of the streetlights, humming like a giant lung.

Inside, Maya flicked on the screens. The building warmed with tech and purpose.

"Sit," she ordered, pointing Jax to a chair.

He raised a brow. "Why?"

She snapped on gloves. "Because you look like you're about to put yourself between Callie and a moving train, and I'm not dealing with cardio tonight."

Callie bit back a smile.

Maya unpacked a med kit. "You're tense. Your shoulder's locked."

"I'm fine," Jax said.

She stabbed a finger at him. "If you break down tomorrow, I'll resuscitate you solely to kill you myself."

Callie laughed — a sound Jax would have walked barefoot over glass to hear again.

"Sit," she echoed.

He sat.

Maya massaged a patch beneath his shoulder blade, sharp and fast.

Jax hissed.

"Oh good, he's alive," Logan said, leaning on the railing above.

"Barely," Maya muttered.

Callie watched the way tension eased from Jax's spine, the way his eyes softened when he finally looked at her.

"You're carrying too much," she said quietly.

"Comes with the job."

"Not all of it does."

He held her gaze.

He didn't argue.

Callie stayed on the mezzanine while the others worked — Logan checking radios, Maya rerouting an emergency signal to Chase's tablet, Jax testing the alarm responses, Chase calibrating a motion sensor that did *not* need more calibration.

She watched them move — five people who had built a fortress out of care and stubbornness.

And somewhere between the cables and the coffee cups and the bad jokes, the fear loosened its grip on her ribs.

She'd found her people.

Or they'd found her.

Maybe both.

And tomorrow — they would stand with her.

Jax came up the stairs, a quiet presence at her side.

"You okay?" he asked.

"Yes."

"No," he said gently. "Truth."

She exhaled. "I'm scared."

"Good."

She blinked. "Good?"

"Fear keeps you alert," he said. "Not weak."

She leaned on the railing, watching the crew below.

"I don't know how to repay all of this."

"You don't."

She frowned. "You're doing all this because...?"

"Because you didn't deserve what happened.

Because someone hurt you and thinks he still can.

Because I would burn half this town down before I let him near you again."

Her breath caught.

He swallowed.

"And because," he added, softer, "I never stopped caring."

The air shifted — warm, fragile, real.

They stood like that until Logan yelled up, "IF ANYONE'S GOING TO HAVE A MOMENT, PLEASE WARN ME SO I CAN PUT EARPLUGS IN."

Jax glared.

Callie laughed.

The tension snapped like an overstretched wire.

Night — Closing the Mill

The Mill was quiet now — screens dimmed, lights low, radios charging.

Callie stood by the door, keys in hand, glancing back at the empty workspace that had become a strange kind of sanctuary.

"You're staying here tonight," Jax said.

She nodded. "I won't be alone?"

"Not for a second."

Logan waved from the couch near the reception desk, blanket over his legs, looking smug. "I've got watch. I promise not to snore. Much."

Maya locked the far door. "We rotate every two hours. You sleep. That's the only rule."

Chase rolled out a sleeping mat nearby. "I volunteered for the shift where I get to eat all the leftover muffins. It's important work."

Callie laughed softly.

A week ago she couldn't have imagined feeling safe anywhere.

Tonight, she felt safe everywhere they stood.

She turned to Jax. "You should rest too."

"I will."

"You won't."

A small smile tugged at his mouth.

"You know me too well."

"Not yet," she said, "but I want to."

Something flickered across his face — hope, fear, relief, all of it tangled.

He stepped a little closer.

"We get through tomorrow," he said, voice low, "and you'll have all the time in the world."

Her heartbeat thudded once — heavy enough that she felt it in her throat.

"Good," she whispered.

Lights dimmed.

Doors locked.

The Mill settled into night, steel walls humming with quiet intent.

Callie lay on the spare cot Chase had assembled, blanket pulled to her chin.

She expected fear to creep back in.

It didn't.

Instead she felt still.

And when she opened her eyes once, just once,

she saw Jax sitting on the metal steps — elbows on knees, watching the door even in half-dark —

and the word that came to her was not *fear*, or *danger*, or *broken*.

It was *home*.

She closed her eyes.

Tomorrow they would confront a shadow.

Tomorrow everything shifted.

Tomorrow someone would finally stumble into the light.

But tonight —

Tonight she slept in a fortress built for her.

And Jax, a silent sentinel with a heartbeat she knew too well, kept watch until dawn.

11

CHAPTER 11 — THE DAY THE TOWN HELD ITS BREATH

Crimson Creek — Morning
  Callie's Café

Morning in Crimson Creek looked almost normal.

Dogs tugged at leashes.

A ute rolled past with music leaking through cracked windows.

Shop signs flipped from CLOSED to OPEN.

And on the corner of Murray Street, Callie wiped down her counters with movements so steady they looked like defiance carved into routine.

Steam curled from the espresso machine.

The chalkboard out front read in soft white strokes:

Open.

Be kind.

We're all trying.

Jax watched from the far corner table, a newspaper open but long unread.

He looked like a tradie on a smoko break — boots dusty, sleeves rolled — but every muscle in his body was tuned to the café door like a held breath.

Callie caught his gaze once.

Her smile was small, but it was there.

"We're doing this," she said quietly when she brought him a coffee.

"We are," he said.

"And I'm fine."

"You are."

"And if I'm not—?"

"I'll see it."

She nodded once, trusting that answer more than she trusted the lock on the front door.

Logan leaned against the trunk of his cruiser, sunglasses on, pretending to eat a banana.

He wasn't fooling anyone — especially not Maya, who had just muttered in his earpiece:

"Try to blend in without looking like you're auditioning for a health PSA."

"I'm a picture of subtlety," he replied.

"You're in aviators, Logan. And a leather jacket."

"Some of us were born iconic."

"Some of us were born annoying."

"I contain multitudes."

His eyes flicked to the café entrance as a woman with a pram walked in.

Normal.

Calm.

Predictable.

Good.

But the air had that pre-storm tension he associated with raids and standoffs — something unseen shifting just beneath the skin of the day.

He tossed the banana peel in a bin.

"Let's keep our pattern loose," he said into the comm. "We want him confident."

"Confidence or arrogance?" Chase asked from his position near the newsagent.

"Same thing in creeps."

◆ ◆ ◆

Callie served three lattes, two muffins, a flat white, and a long black to a local fisherman who always paid in coins.

Her hands didn't shake.

She didn't startle at the bell.

Every movement felt deliberate, like each act of normalcy was a small rebellion.

Chase arrived next, wearing an old denim apron and carrying a clipboard.

"If anyone asks," he said under his breath, "I'm doing a supply audit."

"You blew up the last coffee grinder you touched," she whispered back.

"Which is why I'm doing inventory and absolutely nothing electrical."

He positioned himself near the window fern — the one where they'd found the camera.

His jaw tightened at the memory.

He leaned closer to Callie, voice low. "Just so you know, every time I look at that planter box, I want to set it on fire."

"Same," she whispered.

◆ ◆ ◆

Maya sat in the storeroom with screens arranged like stained-glass windows of surveillance.

The café door, alley, footpath, rooftops, riverwalk — all of it alive, shifting, breathing.

She sipped brutal black coffee and murmured:

"Come on, come on… show me something."

But nothing showed.

Which was somehow worse.

A predator staying still meant a predator thinking.

And the silence in the feeds felt engineered — too neat.

She tapped her comm.

"Jax? You picking up anything?"

"Not yet."

Her fingertips hovered above the keyboard.

"He's watching. I can feel it."

"Same," he said.

Callie's voice floated through the mic two seconds later.

"Then let him watch. Today isn't his."

Maya smiled — small, proud.

"There she is," she whispered.

✦ ✦ ✦

It happened just after eleven.

Callie was steaming milk when the bell over the door chimed — cheerful, harmless, ordinary.

But Jax's head snapped up, eyes narrowing before he even understood why.

The man who walked in was normal on paper:

Mid-thirties.

Cap pulled low.

Work boots.

High-vis shirt.

A takeaway cup from another café in hand.

But he didn't smell like a local.

Didn't move like one either.

He scanned the room — not like someone choosing a pastry, but like someone counting exits.

A thin spark lit behind Jax's ribs. Instinct. Old, sharp, never wrong.

Callie offered her trained smile. "Hi there. What can I get you?"

The man stepped forward.

But his gaze never landed on the menu.

Only on her.

And then — just as quickly — he dropped his eyes to his phone and shuffled

87

backward.

"Sorry. Wrong place," he muttered.

He turned.

Left.

Walked away down the footpath.

Too fast.

"Logan," Jax murmured into the comm. "Tail him."

"Already on it."

Callie's hands tightened around the milk jug. "Is that—?"

"Don't assume anything," Jax said. "But yes. Something's off."

She exhaled slowly through her nose.

"I'm okay."

He nodded.

But didn't believe it.

◆ ◆ ◆

Logan followed the man from a half-block back, sunglasses on, jacket loose.

The guy turned onto Quay Street.

Walked another thirty metres.

Slowed slightly.

Then he paused at a parked ute — opened the driver's door — and got in.

Logan's brows lowered.

"Registration runs clean," Maya murmured into his ear. "Belongs to a plumber in town."

"Does this bloke look like a plumber?"

"Can he hold a wrench?"

"I'll let you know after I introduce him to one."

But as Logan approached —

the ute rolled forward —

turned a corner —

and was gone before he could make the plate.

Logan swore softly.

"He ghosted me," he said.

Maya's voice felt like a cold drop down his spine.

"He knew you were following."

"Yup."

Jax's voice slid in next.

"Eyes up. He's testing our perimeter."

Callie swallowed. "Why now?"

Maya answered before anyone else could.

"Because he wants to know how many shadows are standing between him and you."

◆ ◆ ◆

Callie stood at the coffee station staring at her hands.

They weren't shaking.

But they weren't still either.

Jax approached, dropping his voice. "Talk to me."

"He didn't look like him," she whispered.

"Doesn't mean anything."

"He wasn't the right height. And his shoulders—"

"Callie—"

"I'm not saying it wasn't him. I'm saying there are more eyes on me than just his."

Jax stilled.

Because that was the one truth they hadn't said aloud.

If the stalker wasn't acting alone —

If someone was helping —

If someone was feeding him information —

If this wasn't obsession, but orchestration—

His stomach dropped.

"We're tightening things," he said. "This changes the pattern."

"It changes everything," she corrected softly.

✦ ✦ ✦

She flipped the sign to CLOSED with a hand heavier than she wanted it to be.

The others filtered in as the light died outside — Logan first, then Chase, then Maya.

"Tomorrow," Maya said. "He'll push. Today was recon."

Callie nodded.

She felt it too.

The shift.

The shadow moving closer.

Jax placed a gentle hand on her back.

"You did good today."

She breathed out.

A shaky, tired exhale.

"So did you," she said.

But when she looked up, she realised something:

He wasn't looking at the door.

He was looking at her.

Like she was the first calm morning after a war he'd never learned how to leave.

And she realised something else:

She'd stopped being afraid of that.

✦ ✦ ✦

They walked back to the Mill together through the cooling dusk.

"Tomorrow," he murmured, "we finish this."

She nodded.

But her voice was barely a breath when she asked:

"Jax? If tomorrow goes wrong..."

"It won't."

"But if it does—"

"It won't," he repeated. "Because I'm not losing you again."

90

Her breath caught.

Their steps slowed.

"Look at me," he said quietly.

She did.

And the world stilled around them.

"I'm here," he whispered. "All the way until this ends."

Her voice trembled.

"But what if *you* get hurt?"

He stepped closer, almost touching her forehead with his.

"Then I heal.

Then I stand back up.

Then I keep going.

Because I don't stop where you're involved."

The night hummed around them.

And for the first time since this began, she believed him without hesitation.

"Okay," she whispered.

And his answering smile — small, worn, real — was the most dangerous thing she'd ever felt.

Because it changed everything she thought she knew about the man she'd once lost.

Tomorrow —

the real hunt began.

12

CHAPTER 12 — CROSSHAIRS

Crimson Creek — Dawn
Pegasus Mill

The sky was a sheet of pale silver when Jax unlocked the Mill door, the world still tasting of night.

Cold air rushed in first, carrying the scent of wet metal and river silt.

Callie stepped inside behind him, shoulders squared, chin lifted — the posture of someone refusing to bend.

She'd slept maybe two hours.

He'd slept none.

She moved toward the counter near the workstation.

He watched her in that quiet, careful way he had — like she was both fragile and unbreakable at once.

"Coffee?" she asked.

"God, yes."

She smiled faintly. "Thought so."

✦ ✦ ✦

Pegasus Briefing — 06:12

Logan arrived first, a sausage roll between his teeth and a file under his arm.

"Morning, family," he said, dropping into a chair.

"Define family," Maya muttered, entering right behind him with her laptop already open.

"People I'm stuck with despite my best efforts," Logan said.

Chase ducked through the door next, hair still wet from a too-fast shower, carrying two travel mugs and a USB drive between his teeth.

Jax scanned them all.

"Okay," he said. "Overnight movement?"

Maya pushed her glasses up. "Council cameras caught a man matching the height and build of the café visitor. But he avoided all facial angles. Like he knew exactly where they were."

Logan flipped open his file. "Plumber ute was stolen. Found dumped near the south creek. Wiped. Clean."

"Of course it was," Chase muttered.

Jax looked at Callie.

She swallowed hard but stayed steady.

"What does that mean?" she asked.

Maya answered gently. "It means yesterday wasn't him slipping up. It was him *introducing himself*. Testing response time. Testing your heartbeat."

Logan leaned back. "Testing our footprint."

Jax exhaled slowly.

"We expected this. Today he pushes harder."

"And we push back harder," Logan said, cracking his knuckles.

Maya moved to the map wall, tapping a red marker on the café district.

"We tighten the net.

Two at the café.

One cross-street.

One river walk.

And Chase here—" she pointed the marker at him "—is going to take a stroll with a fake package."

Chase blinked. "A stroll?"

"You're our bait," Logan said cheerfully.

Chase groaned. "Why am I always the bait?"

"Because you're adorable and harmless-looking," Maya replied.

"I have a black belt!"

"In judo," Logan said. "Which is adorable."

Callie tried not to laugh — and failed.

Maya circled the river district.

"If he's watching, he'll react to new movement. We want him curious. Curious people slip."

Jax folded his arms.

"What about Callie?" he asked.

Maya held his gaze.

"She stays inside public view at all times. Staff around her. Customers around her. No blind spots."

Callie crossed her arms. "I'm not a china figurine."

"No," Maya said softly. "You're a lightning rod. Big difference."

Jax took a breath.

"Today, you don't walk alone. Not even three steps."

Callie didn't argue.

That scared him more than if she had.

✦ ✦ ✦

07:30 — *The Walk to the Café*

The sun hadn't yet decided what kind of day it wanted to be — that half-mist, half-gold light that makes everything look innocent.

Jax walked beside Callie in silence, alert but pretending not to be.

Her fingers brushed his once.

He didn't pull away.

"Big day," she murmured.

"It'll go our way."

"You sound certain."

"I am certain."

They crossed the street.

The café sign swung gently in the breeze.

Callie unlocked the door.

The familiar smell hit instantly — coffee beans, baked sugar, warm wood.

But underneath: a thread of unease.

Not from the room — from *her*.

"Breathe," Jax said quietly.

She did.

Customers trickled in within minutes — early risers, tradies, a schoolteacher in bright sneakers.

Logan took a seat near the window with a newspaper.

Maya set up at the corner table with her laptop.

Chase lingered by the planter box, pretending to adjust the chalkboard.

A net woven from people and poise.

All they needed was a tug.

❖ ❖ ❖

08:22 — *First Contact*

It came with the simplest thing:

A text.

Callie's phone lit up on the counter:

UNKNOWN NUMBER.

She froze.

Jax appeared beside her like a shadow.

"Don't touch it," he said.

Maya was there in three strides.

She tapped the screen with a stylus.

A preview appeared:

Red looks better.

But you always knew that.

Callie's breath stopped.
   Jax's jaw went iron-hard.
   Maya opened the message to trace it.
   More words appeared.

Step two.

Right on time.

Then:

Smile for me.

Callie looked up instinctively — too fast.
   Jax caught her chin lightly, guiding her gaze back down.
   "No," he murmured. "Don't give him the view."
   But it was too late.
   The bell over the door chimed.
   A perfectly ordinary man walked in — jeans, jacket, hoodie up — ordering a flat white and sitting in the far corner like anyone else.
   But when Callie lowered her eyes, she saw his reflection in the steel milk jug.
   He wasn't watching his phone.
   He wasn't watching the door.
   He wasn't watching the menu.
   He was watching **her**.
   Jax moved first.
   Logan second.
   Maya third.

Like a trained choreography.

✦ ✦ ✦

Jax reached the table.

"Morning," he said casually.

The man looked up.

Too calm.

Too collected.

"Can I help you?" he asked in a pleasant voice.

Jax leaned on the edge of the table.

"We'd like a word."

"Who's we?" the man asked.

Logan pulled out the chair opposite him.

Maya stood behind, arms folded.

"Oh," the man said softly.

"That kind of we."

Callie hovered near the counter, trying to breathe.

Jax spoke first.

"Why are you here?"

"Coffee?" the man offered.

Maya's tone sharpened. "Your phone. Put it on the table."

He did — smiling like this was a game.

"Unlock it," she said.

"No."

Logan leaned forward. "Mate, you want to do this the easy way or the annoying way?"

The man shrugged. "I'm just drinking."

But Jax could see it — the pulse at the man's jaw, the flicker in his eyes, the hitch of breath when Callie shifted her weight.

Not the stalker.

But something adjacent.

Something assisting.

"Look at me," Jax said.

The man's gaze slid over.

"You're not here by accident."

"No one is," he said quietly.

"We all play our part."

"Whose part is yours?" Jax asked.

"Messenger," he said.

"From who?"

He smiled.

Then whispered:

"You already know his name."

Jax lunged —

but the man slammed his leg into the table, scattering cups, sending Logan stumbling sideways.

He bolted toward the door.

"CHASE!" Maya shouted.

Chase was already on the move, sprinting across the street.

But the man reached the footpath, ducked behind a passing truck, and—

Gone.

Just... gone.

Vanished into the morning air like he'd never been there.

Callie's hands shook for the first time since the Mill.

"He was watching me," she whispered.

Jax stepped to her side, close enough to shield her from the windows.

"No," he said.

"He was letting us know we're being watched."

Her pulse thundered.

"So what now?"

Jax exhaled, eyes narrowing — soldier-brain cutting into place.

"Now?" he said.

"We hunt the messenger."

"But the real threat... he's close, isn't he?"

Jax nodded once.

"He's here," he whispered.

"In Crimson Creek.

And today he wanted you to feel it."

Callie swallowed.

Then squared her shoulders.

"Then let's make him regret that."

Jax couldn't help it —

his chest warmed in a way that felt dangerous.

And the day shifted.

Not into chaos —

but into clarity.

The rules had changed.

Today wasn't about surviving.

Today was about strategy.

The stalker wasn't playing hide-and-seek anymore.

He was playing **possession**.

And Pegasus had just been forced to move to offense.

13

CHAPTER 13 — THE MAN WHO STOOD TOO STILL

Crimson Creek — Late Morning
   The Café

The place felt wrong in the minutes after the messenger vanished.
   Not loud-wrong.
   Not chaotic-wrong.
   Just... shifted.
   Like the walls had leaned in to listen.
   Logan slammed the door shut and flipped the lock.
   "Okay," he said, breathing hard. "Someone tell me why random Hoodie McSmugface just delivered a cryptic monologue and dipped like a magician."
   Maya didn't answer immediately — she was scrolling through the man's forgotten coffee cup, searching for prints, DNA, anything.
   "There's residue on the rim," she murmured. "Skin cells. Enough for a profile."
   "That's something," Chase said, pacing.
   "It's something," she agreed, "but it's not everything."
   "What's everything?" Callie asked, voice steady but eyes too bright.
   Maya lifted her head.

"That he knew exactly how to get close without touching you."

Callie's jaw tightened.

"So what happens now?"

Jax stepped to her side.

"We change the rules."

He glanced at Maya.

"Full perimeter expansion."

She nodded. "On it."

Jax turned to Logan.

"You take the river walk. Chase — rooftops and alley cams. I'll take the workshop district."

"Got it," Logan said.

Chase saluted. "Copy."

"And me?" Callie asked.

Jax's eyes met hers.

"Stay where people are."

Her chin lifted. "I'm not hiding."

"I'm not asking you to hide," he said softly.

"I'm asking you to not walk into the dark alone."

Her breath faltered for a heartbeat.

Then she nodded.

❖ ❖ ❖

He moved with the kind of walk that stayed between a prowl and a march — boots silent on cracked pavement, shoulders loose but coiled.

Crimson Creek's old industrial precinct always smelled like sun-warmed metal and leftover storms. Today, it smelled like something else:

Old sweat.

Dust.

And the faintest trace of burnt paper.

He followed it to an abandoned workshop used for Council storage.

Cameras showed activity here last night — movement that didn't match wildlife, wind, or cars.

He approached the side door slowly, testing the handle.

Unlocked.

Inside, the air was stale and cool.

Sunlight slipped through broken panels, painting long bars of gold across the concrete floor.

Something glinted.

He crouched.

A silver coin.

No — not a coin.

A **pressed token**.

Thin metal stamped with a stylised wolf's head.

A wolf with its eyes scratched out.

Jax's fingers closed around it.

His pulse dropped low and cold.

"Found something," he said into his comm.

"Define something," Logan replied.

"Marker," Jax said. "He left a marker."

Maya's voice sharpened. "For you?"

"For Callie," Jax answered.

Then he noticed it — faint footprints near the back door.

Smaller than his.

Same as the mezzanine at the Mill.

The stalker had been here recently.

Maybe last night.

Maybe this morning.

Maybe both.

Jax exhaled through his teeth.

The game wasn't widening.

It was tightening.

✦ ✦ ✦

Callie stood behind the counter as the café filled with lunchtime regulars.

Small talk.

Coffee orders.

The clink of cups.

Normal life.

But her eyes kept drifting to the windows.

The street.

Every reflection.

Every silhouette.

She wiped the counter for the seventh time.

"Callie."

She looked up.

Maya stood beside her, voice low.

"I've isolated the message origin. It came from a mobile repeater — one that's on the move."

"Meaning?"

"Meaning he's circling."

Callie's stomach tightened.

"Here?"

"Within a kilometre."

A customer approached the counter and smiled politely — a woman in her early twenties with a cardigan and a messy bun.

Ordinary.

Friendly.

"What can I get you?" Callie asked.

As she turned to the machine, the woman leaned closer to Maya and whispered:

"He's been outside. In the alley. The man in the jacket."

Maya's head snapped around.

"When?"

"About ten minutes ago. I thought he was waiting for someone, but he didn't move. Just stood there. Not blinking."

Callie's breath caught.

"Is he still there?" Maya asked.

The woman hesitated.

"I... don't know. I didn't want to look again."

Maya squeezed her arm. "Thank you. You did the right thing."

Callie placed the woman's cup on the counter with shaking hands.

Not fear.

Just adrenaline.

"He's close," she whispered.

Maya nodded once.

"Yes. And he's getting bold."

Callie's eyes drifted to the alley door.

If he was standing out there...

If he'd been there for minutes...

Then he'd been listening.

Watching.

Breathing the same air.

Callie wiped her palms on her apron.

"He wants me to see him," she said.

"No," Maya replied softly.

"He wants you to **feel** him before you see him."

Callie swallowed.

"That's worse."

Maya didn't disagree.

✦ ✦ ✦

The river glimmered gold, water moving slow and thick.

Logan walked beside it with the easy saunter of a man who had absolutely no reason to be suspicious.

Internally, he was a razor.

His gaze trailed every pedestrian, every bench, every car parked along the railings.

Then — movement on the far bank.

104

A man stood facing the water.

Still.

Too still.

He had one hand in his pocket, head slightly tilted like he was listening to something deep underground.

Logan slowed.

"Possible visual," he murmured.

"Where?" Jax asked immediately.

"River bend. Far bank. About one-sixty metres."

"Description?"

"Six foot. Average build. Tan jacket. Not moving. Not acknowledging anyone. Just... standing."

"Do not approach," Maya said sharply.

"I'm not approaching," Logan replied.

"I'm observing."

The man on the far bank didn't shift.

Didn't look up.

Didn't react to passing joggers.

But Logan noticed something.

The man's line of sight was angled slightly downward — toward the water.

Toward the mirror surface.

Which reflected...

The street behind Logan.

"Ah, hell," he muttered.

"He's using the water as a mirror."

"Meaning?" Callie's voice slipped through the channel.

"He can see the café street," Logan said. "Perfect angle."

"Can he see me?" she asked.

Logan hesitated.

Then:

"...Yes."

Silence.

Then Callie whispered:

"Then he's watching right now."

Logan steadied his breath.

"And that, Red Wolf, means we've got him right where we want him."

Because now — finally — they had a physical visual.

A real one.

A target.

But when Logan blinked—

The man was gone.

No footsteps.

No movement.

Just absence — clean as a cut.

"Shit," Logan whispered.

"Lost him."

✦ ✦ ✦

12:41 PM

The café emptied around midday.

Workers returning to offices.

Kids heading home for lunch.

Callie leaned against the counter, breath shallow.

She felt him.

Not saw.

Not heard.

Felt.

A presence pressing against the day.

Jax re-entered the café, jaw hard.

"Logan lost him," he said. "He vanished near the bridge."

Maya added, "The repeater signal just jumped again. He's moving faster."

Chase burst through the back door.

"Guys," he panted.

"You need to see this."

They followed him out the rear door into the alley behind the café.

And froze.

Someone had written something on the wall.

Not paint.

Not marker.

Ash.

Burnt paper rubbed into the stone.

Five words, smeared in dark grey.

YOU WALKED PAST ME TODAY

Callie's throat closed.

Jax stepped in front of her, blocking the wall from view even though she'd already read it.

"Don't touch anything," he snapped.

Logan swore under his breath.

Maya photographed it.

Chase scanned for prints.

Callie wrapped her arms around herself.

"He was here," she whispered.

"Here in the alley while I was inside."

"Not just here," Maya said softly.

"He was so close he felt you pass."

Callie's eyes burned.

"I didn't see him."

"You weren't supposed to," Jax said.

She looked up at him — eyes wet but fierce.

"He wanted me to know I missed him."

Jax cupped her cheek, thumb brushing away a tear she hadn't noticed.

"You didn't miss him," he said quietly.

"Then why write that?"

"So you think you're losing ground," Jax answered.

"And he can step ahead."

Callie nodded.

"So he's controlling the narrative."

"Not anymore," Jax said.

He turned to the team.

"We treat this like a countdown.

He's escalating.

He's close.

And today—"

His voice dropped into something cold and final.

"—today he made a mistake."

Callie whispered:

"What mistake?"

Jax looked at her.

"He stood still long enough for us to see the shape of him."

And the next step became clear:

They weren't waiting anymore.

They were hunting.

14

CHAPTER 14 — THE NAME HE SHOULDN'T KNOW

Crimson Creek — Afternoon
Behind the Café

The ash-smudged message stayed on the wall long after the team stepped back inside.

YOU WALKED PAST ME TODAY.

Callie couldn't unsee it.

The shape of each letter.

The way the burnt paper had smeared like someone had ground it in with their thumb.

Every stroke meant:

I was close enough to touch you.

Inside the café, she washed her hands three times, scrubbing until her skin went pink.

Jax watched from the doorway.

His arms were crossed, but his shoulders were too tense to be anything but barely restrained fury.

"You don't have to do that," he said quietly.

"It makes me feel better."

"Does it?"

"No," she admitted. "But it makes me feel like I'm doing something."

He stepped forward and turned off the tap.

Her breath caught — he was too close, heat radiating off him, his presence grounding her in ways she didn't want to look at too closely.

"You *are* doing something," he said.

"You're still standing here."

She swallowed.

"That's not bravery. That's adrenaline."

"No," he said softly.

"Bravery is choosing to breathe when your instincts tell you to run."

For a moment, the only sound was the water dripping from her fingers into the stainless-steel sink.

Then the comms in Jax's pocket crackled.

"Jax, you need to get out here."

Logan.

Breathless.

Jax straightened immediately.

"Where?" he asked.

"Out front. Now."

He left the kitchen at a run.

Callie followed, heart thudding.

✦ ✦ ✦

Logan stood on the footpath, staring at something taped to the café's front window.

A photograph.

Printed.

Recent.

Crisp.

Callie's stomach lurched.

Jax ripped it off the glass.

110

It was a photo of Callie standing in the alley earlier — staring at the ash-written message — with Jax in front of her, blocking most of the view.

But the angle was wrong.

This photo wasn't taken from the street.

Not from a window.

Not from a camera Chase would have noticed.

It was from *above*.

As though someone had been on a rooftop.

Watching.

Listening.

Waiting.

Maya arrived, breath sharp.

"Let me see—"

Jax handed her the picture.

She scanned it once, then twice, then again slower.

"This angle..." she murmured.

Chase appeared next.

"It's from the roof of the florist next door," he said.

"No other vantage point matches this height."

Logan swore. "I checked that roof ten minutes ago."

"Which means he was already gone by the time you got there," Maya said.

Callie's breath trembled.

"He watched us find the ash message," she whispered. "He was right there."

Jax clenched his jaw.

The muscle ticked hard.

Logan frowned.

"What's that on the back?"

Jax flipped the photo over.

A sentence scrawled in red ink:

CALLIE JAMES ALWAYS DID LIKE TO BE FOLLOWED

Callie staggered back as though shoved.

Her middle name.

Her **full** name.

The only people who used it—

Her mother.

Her father.

Jax.

And one other.

Her pulse spiked.

"He knows my *middle name*," she whispered.

Jax caught her before she hit the wall.

"Hey," he murmured, steadying her.

"Look at me."

Her eyes lifted to his.

"That's not possible," she said. "No one uses that name. I haven't used it since…"

"Since your mother," Jax finished softly.

She nodded, barely holding herself together.

Maya stepped forward, voice gentler than any of them had heard all day.

"Callie," she said carefully.

"Is there *anyone* from your past — anyone who would know that name — who could be doing this?"

Callie's face went still.

Her eyes unfocused.

And then something inside her broke loose.

Her voice cracked.

"Jax… he said something once. Someone from town. Years ago. I thought it was nothing but—"

"Who?" Jax asked.

She shook her head. "No. It can't be. He moved away. I haven't seen him since—"

"Who?" Jax repeated, firmer now.

Logan's voice softened.

"No judgement, Red Wolf. Just the truth."

Callie closed her eyes, inhaling once.

And then she whispered a single name.

A quiet name.

A name that made Jax stop breathing.

Because he knew it.

He had known it for years.

A name from the past.

A name from the funeral.

A name from the night before he left.

Callie whispered:

"Evan."

The street went dead silent.

Logan turned slowly.

"No. No way. Evan Ward? The kid who used to hang around after school?"

Callie nodded.

"He was harmless," Logan said, frowning.

"No," Jax said quietly.

"He wasn't."

Callie looked at him sharply.

"What do you mean?"

Jax exhaled through his teeth, long and slow.

"Your mum asked me to keep an eye on him," he said. "She didn't trust him around you."

Callie froze.

"What? Why didn't you tell me?"

"You were sixteen," he said.

"And you had enough grief in your chest that year."

Her breath hitched.

"He moved away. Brisbane. Years ago. He's not— he can't be—"

Maya stepped in.

"People don't always move on just because you do."

Callie shook her head.

"No. Evan was quiet. Awkward. Shy. He wasn't—"

"He used to stand outside the library after your shifts," Jax said quietly.

"You never noticed. I did."

Callie's knees went weak.

Jax caught her again.

"Stay with me," he murmured. "Right here."

She clutched his shirt.

"You think it's Evan?" she whispered.

Jax didn't answer immediately.

Because the truth had settled in his gut like a stone.

"He knew your middle name," Jax said softly.

"And he was obsessed with anything connected to your mum."

Callie's eyes filled with a slow, creeping horror.

"But Evan left town," she whispered.

"Doesn't mean he forgot you," Logan said.

Jax's voice dropped into something dark and deadly.

"I'll talk to the Wards."

Callie grabbed his hand.

"No. Jax. If it's him—"

"If it's him," Jax said, "I find him before he gets any closer."

She swallowed.

"What if he's not working alone?"

Jax met her eyes.

"Then we hunt the second man, too."

Callie's voice trembled.

"Jax... I'm scared."

He lifted her chin, brushing his thumb across her cheek in a gesture he didn't even try to hide.

"I know," he said softly.

"And you're not alone in it."

She leaned into him.

Just enough for him to feel it.

And everything in him tightened.

Logan cleared his throat.

"Okay, well, that's definitely a conversation we're coming back to—"

Maya elbowed him hard.

Chase whispered loudly, "Let them have a moment!"

Jax ignored them all.

He kept his eyes on Callie.

"We're ending this," he whispered.

"No more hints. No more messages. No more watching."

"How?" she asked.

"By doing the one thing he doesn't expect."

"Which is?"

Jax said it like a vow:

"We stop reacting.

And we start hunting."

15

CHAPTER 15 — THE VISITOR IN THE DARK

Crimson Creek — Evening
   Pegasus Mill

Night settled over the Mill in a way that didn't feel like darkness so much as pressure.

The kind that gathers in the ribs.

The kind that warns you something is coming.

The team clustered around the main table, the photograph of Callie and the message on the back placed dead centre like evidence and accusation both.

Callie kept her arms wrapped around herself. Jax stood close enough to steady her without touching her. The rest of the team moved with a kind of quiet violence — minds sharpening, jaws tight.

"He watched from the roof," Maya repeated, scanning the grid of street cams. "He didn't just follow. He studied."

"That's escalation," Logan said flatly. "He's done hiding. He wants her to *feel* it."

Callie swallowed hard. "He used my full name. Evan is—was—the only person besides my mum who ever used it."

Jax's voice dropped into that tone he used when the soldier stepped forward.

"We're not assuming Evan yet."

"Why not?" Callie whispered.

Jax looked at her, and the truth in his eyes made her chest tighten.

"Because this is smarter than the boy we knew," he said quietly.

"This is someone patient. Strategic. Someone who knows how to disappear into the gaps."

Callie took a shaky breath.

"Then who?"

Nobody answered.

Because nobody knew.

Logan broke the silence, pacing.

"We need to talk to Evan. Tonight."

Callie shook her head. "He doesn't live here anymore. He moved—"

"We'll start with his parents," Jax said. "Someone will know where he is."

Chase looked up from the live-feed board.

"And if Evan didn't write that name?"

Jax's jaw flexed. "Then someone else did."

Callie closed her eyes.

"Someone who knows more about me than I realised."

Jax stepped closer, lifting her chin with just two fingers.

"Whoever he is," he said softly, "he's making mistakes now. Messages. Photos. Rooftops. Close contact. That's not confidence. That's unraveling. He's getting sloppy."

A tear escaped her. She didn't bother to hide it.

"Why does that not make me feel better?" she whispered.

"Because you're human," he said.

"And he's a coward."

His thumb brushed her cheek once before he seemed to remember where they were, pulling back just enough.

Maya kept her eyes on the screens but her voice was gentler.

"Callie... there's something else."

Everyone turned.

She brought up the ash-scrawled message:

YOU WALKED PAST ME TODAY.

"Look at the width of the strokes," Maya said. "The pressure. The indentation."

Callie frowned. "What about it?"

Maya zoomed closer.

"The person who wrote that wasn't writing from memory. He was writing what he *felt*."

Logan stared. "Meaning?"

"Meaning he wasn't just close physically," Maya said.

"He was close emotionally."

A cold ripple moved through the room.

Chase whispered it first:

"Someone she knows now."

Callie's breath caught.

Someone here. Someone she greeted. Someone she'd smiled at.

The thought made her dizzy.

Jax's voice snapped like a command:

"Stop."

Everyone froze.

"We don't guess," he said. "We don't blame ghosts. We build the board and we follow facts."

He looked at Callie again, and the promise in his gaze was almost violent in its intensity.

"I'm not losing you," he said softly.

"Not again."

Her heart clenched painfully.

"Then don't run this time," she whispered.

The air between them shifted — thicker, charged, unbearably human.

Logan coughed loudly. "Okay, well—moving right along."

Maya elbowed him without looking.

"Everyone gets one break tonight," she said. "Then we work until we know."

✦ ✦ ✦

Jax and Logan took the ute.

Callie wanted to come.

Jax said no.

It wasn't a request.

"Stay with Maya," he told her. "We'll handle this."

"But—"

"I need you safe," he said, quiet enough she almost missed it.

Callie watched the ute roll out of the yard, taillights disappearing into the dusk, and tried to shake the sense that the night itself was leaning closer.

Inside the Mill, Maya kept the feeds alive while Chase checked pressure sensors and motion alerts.

"You doing okay?" Maya asked.

"No," Callie said. "But I'm not falling apart."

"Good," Maya said simply. "Because falling apart is boring. You're not."

It almost made Callie smile.

Almost.

Then the radio crackled.

Logan's voice.

Tight. Too tight.

"Maya, we've got something."

Callie froze.

"What?" Maya asked.

Static.

Then Logan again:

"Ward house is empty. Been empty a long time."

Callie's pulse spiked.

"But—" she began.

Jax's voice cut through, quiet and sharp like a knife.

"There's more."

"What?" Maya demanded.

A long pause.

Then:

"There are photographs here. Hundreds. In boxes. Sorted. Labelled."

Chase's head snapped up. "Of what?"

Jax answered.

"Callie."

The breath left her lungs like a punch.

"No," she whispered. "No. Evan wasn't—he wasn't like that—"

"Callie," Jax said, softer now, "he's been watching you for years."

A cold wash moved through her bones.

Maya met her eyes.

"I need you to sit down," she said gently.

Callie didn't. She couldn't.

Jax spoke again.

"We're bringing the boxes back. Don't touch anything. Don't go outside. And Callie?"

She swallowed.

"Yes?"

"We're closing the trap tonight."

Callie's voice shook.

"Why?"

Jax answered without hesitation.

"Because he's getting closer.

And I'm done waiting for him to reach you."

The line went dead.

Callie stared at the silent radio, her heartbeat echoing in her ears.

The photograph in the café.

The ash message.

The middle name.

And now this.

Someone had been building a story around her for years. Someone who believed she was part of it. Someone who believed she owed him a role.

Maya moved closer and placed a steady hand between her shoulder blades.

"Breathe," she murmured. "You're not alone."

But Callie wasn't sure breathing was possible anymore.

Because somewhere out there — in the dark beyond the mill doors — someone who knew her name was waiting.

And he wasn't watching from a distance anymore.

He was coming.

Tonight.

16

CHAPTER 16 — THE BOXES HE KEPT

Pegasus Mill — Nightfall

The ute returned with the sound of tyres rolling over wet gravel, muted but unmistakable. Chase was at the door before Logan even braked, and Maya slid the loading bay open halfway, unwilling to give the street a full view of anything happening inside.

Jax stepped out first, a cardboard box in his arms.

Not new.

Not wet.

Kept.

Tended.

Organised.

Logan followed with two more.

Callie's breath turned cold.

She backed up instinctively as they carried the boxes toward the centre table. Jax saw it immediately.

"If you don't want to see this, you don't have to," he said quietly.

She shook her head.

"I do."

He didn't try to argue.

He just set the first box down gently, as though the contents were fragile.

They weren't fragile.

They were horrifying.

Maya pulled on gloves, snapped them at the wrist, and opened the lid.

The room exhaled together.

Inside lay stacks of photographs — some printed at chemists, some cheap home-ink prints, some grainy polaroid-style shots.

All of them of Callie.

Some from years ago.

Some recent.

Some from angles that made her stomach twist — the back of her head, her hands counting change at the counter, her hair blowing in the wind walking to her car.

These weren't random snapshots.

They were curated.

Chase whispered, "Jesus…"

Logan rubbed the back of his neck. "This is not the Evan I remember."

Callie stood frozen. The world narrowed to a point of discomfort just behind her ribs.

Jax lifted the next box.

Inside were notebooks.

He frowned, opening one carefully.

Pages of handwriting, tight and slanted.

He read the first line before he realised what it was.

"Callie James walked past me today. She didn't see me. She hasn't seen me in years, not the way she used to. But she will."

Callie pressed a hand to her mouth.

Maya's eyes burned. "This is obsession in long form. Documented. Chronic. Years of delusion."

Jax closed the notebook like closing a wound.

Callie whispered, "He was… writing a diary about me."

"Not a diary," Maya corrected softly.

"A manifesto."

Callie's heart pounded so hard she felt nauseous.

"There's more," Logan said, opening the third box.

This one was worse.

Inside were objects.

A ribbon from a local charity stall she'd organised seven years ago.

A receipt from her café the week it opened.

A napkin she'd dropped outside the bakery.

A grocery list written in her handwriting — stolen from the trolley at some point.

And most chilling — the red hair clip she'd lost on the day of her mother's memorial service.

Her knees buckled.

Jax moved instantly, catching her under the arms.

"You're okay," he murmured, voice low and fierce. "I've got you."

The words broke something in her.

Not fear.

Not grief.

Something older.

Something tied to the boy he used to be and the man he'd tried not to become again.

She looked up at him.

"This is my fault," she whispered.

He flinched. "No. Absolutely not."

"I should have seen—"

"There was nothing to see," he said, louder now. "He hid it. Carefully. Obsessed minds hide better than sane ones."

She looked at the boxes.

"No one hides this well by accident."

Jax's grip tightened.

"Exactly. Which means he's been preparing for this longer than we realised."

Maya's voice snapped their attention back.

"Guys... there's something else."

She held a bundle of torn envelopes.

Most were blank.

One was not.

One had a date.

A date circled in red ink, written in a careful, ritualistic hand.

27 November.

Callie's breath caught.

"That's—"

"Tomorrow," Maya finished.

The room went dead still.

Chase's fingers froze over the keyboard.

Logan stopped moving entirely.

Even Jax seemed carved into place.

Callie swallowed hard.

"What happens tomorrow?"

Maya showed them the envelope.

Inside was a single line:

WHEN YOU COME HOME.

Jax's face darkened, the kind of expression that meant violence was already being calculated behind the eyes.

Maya continued.

"There's more. Look where the edges are worn. He's handled this one a lot. This date means something to him."

Callie pressed trembling fingers to her temples.

"Tomorrow is the anniversary of my mum's death."

Everything in the room shifted.

Chase swore under his breath.

Logan's jaw worked like he wanted to break something.

Maya's eyes softened — grief recognising grief.

Jax was utterly still.

Callie whispered:

"He thinks I'm going to go to the memorial garden. I do every year."

Jax said nothing for a long moment.

Then:

"He's not meeting you there."

Callie looked up. "What?"

"He's not meeting you there," Jax repeated, voice low and certain. "We are meeting him."

Her breath stuttered.

"You want to use me as bait," she said quietly.

"No," he said, stepping closer.

"I want to use his fantasy as bait. There's a difference."

"A fine one," Maya muttered.

Callie shook her head. "He'll be watching."

"Let him," Jax said.

Logan pointed to the boxes. "He's been building toward this for years. Tomorrow is his finish line."

Callie closed her eyes.

"And you want me to stand at it."

Jax's hand brushed hers, barely there, but grounding.

"You won't be standing alone."

She breathed through her teeth, shaking.

"You want me to walk into the one place where he knows I'll be vulnerable."

"No," he said. "I want you to walk into the one place where *we* control every angle, every escape, every inch of ground."

"And if he doesn't show?"

Jax exhaled slowly.

"He'll show," he said.

"Because he's been waiting for tomorrow longer than we have."

Callie stared at the boxes.

The photos.

The notebooks.

The mementos he shouldn't have.

And for the first time since this started, something fierce began to rise beneath her fear.

Resolve.

If tomorrow was going to be the day—

Then she refused to meet it shaking.

She straightened.

"Okay," she said, voice steadying.

"Then we do it."

Jax blinked.

"Callie—"

"No," she said. "I'm not running anymore."

Her hands smoothed across the steel table as she looked at them one by one.

"Tomorrow morning," she said.

"I go to the memorial garden."

Logan nodded once.

Maya closed her laptop.

Chase began pulling up the map of the garden.

Jax stepped closer.

"Callie," he said quietly. "Look at me."

She did.

"If anything goes wrong—anything—"

"It won't," she said, interrupting him gently.

"Because you'll be there."

His breath hitched before he caught it.

"Always," he said.

And for the first time all day, she believed him.

17

CHAPTER 17 — THE MEMORIAL MORNING

Crimson Creek — Dawn
   Callie's Flat

The morning of the anniversary broke clear and deceptively gentle—sky brushed pale gold, a quiet breeze slipping under the blinds, the kind of dawn that pretended the world was simple.

Callie sat at the edge of her bed, hair unbrushed, hands clasped around a ribbon she hadn't opened in years.

Her mother's.

Soft satin.

Faded pink.

Every year, she tied it around the tree at the memorial garden.

Every year, she whispered the same promise: *I'm trying, Mum. I'm still trying.*

Her throat tightened.

Today that promise would be witnessed by a man who didn't deserve to be anywhere near her mother's memory.

She closed her fingers hard around the ribbon and exhaled.

A knock sounded—three taps, firm, familiar.

Jax.

She opened the door and found him already reading the room—the tightened jaw, the clutter on the bedside table, the weight of grief she hadn't quite learned to carry right.

"You okay?" he asked quietly.

"No," she answered honestly. "But I'm not broken."

He nodded, accepting the truth without pity.

"Ready?"

"Almost."

He watched as she slid the ribbon into her jacket pocket.

"You don't have to do this alone," he said.

She met his eyes.

"I'm not."

That earned the smallest tilt of his mouth, something warm but restrained—the man holding the soldier in check.

"You packed?" he asked.

She gestured to the small satchel on the chair. "Phone, water, spare key, jacket."

"And the alarm Chase gave you?"

She tapped the thin device clipped to her belt.

"One press for Pegasus. Two for police. Three for the apocalypse."

"Good," he murmured.

She hesitated.

"You think he's going to show?"

Jax didn't soften the truth.

"Yes."

She breathed through the dread, letting it move instead of lock.

Jax extended his hand—not to touch, but to steady the moment.

"Then we're ready," he said.

And for once, she believed him completely.

Pegasus Mill — Thirty Minutes Later

The team moved like gears in a well-oiled machine—quiet, fast, precise.

Logan loaded a duffel with gear: comms, emergency med kit, restraints, evidence bags, an extra sidearm.

Chase had three screens open, mapping sightlines across the memorial garden.

"South gate's our best entry point," he said. "Tall hedges. Good cover. Cameras on the path will be disguised as bird boxes."

Maya pulled her hair into a knot, jaw tight.

"I'll run overwatch from here. Audio open on all channels. Jax, Logan—you'll be on foot, staggered wide."

Callie stepped closer.

"Where will I be?"

"Centre path," Maya said. "At the tree. Exactly like you would any other year."

Callie swallowed.

"He's expecting that."

"Good," Logan said. "The trap works better when he thinks he's choreographing it."

Callie rubbed her thumb along the ribbon in her pocket.

"What if he comes from behind?" she asked.

"He won't," Maya said. "He needs you to see him. That's part of the fantasy."

Jax's eyes flicked to the door.

"We leave in five."

Callie nodded, but a question tugged at her.

"And if Evan isn't the one we meet today?"

Silence.

Jax stepped closer until his voice dropped to something only she heard.

"Then whoever it is," he said, "they've already made their last mistake."

Her breath caught.

He looked at her like she was the only anchor left in a storm.

"Stay with me," he said.

"I am," she whispered.

He nodded once, something hard and certain settling behind his eyes.

Crimson Creek — 9:12 a.m.

The town felt unnaturally quiet as they drove the back streets—shops opening slowly, school run thinning, the river carrying its slow brown weight under the bridge.

Jax pulled off two streets short of the garden and killed the engine.

"We go on foot from here."

Callie's heartbeat rose.

Logan slid out first, scanning the street with a casual confidence that didn't match the lock of his grip on the strap of his bag.

Jax held the door open for Callie.

"You ready?"

"Ask me again in ten seconds."

They walked.

The memorial garden sat behind the council chambers, a crescent-shaped grove of native trees and small plaques set in stone. Morning sunlight filtered through the branches, scattering gold across the gravel path.

Callie's boots crunched softly.

Every sound felt magnified.

Every shadow felt aware.

Jax flanked her left. Logan walked ahead at a distance that looked normal but was strategically perfect.

Callie spotted the tree before she reached it—the one she visited every year. A eucalypt with broad arms, bark peeling in soft curls, the trunk marked by ribbons faded by time.

Her breath trembled.

"This is it," she whispered.

Jax touched her elbow once—steady, grounding.

"We're with you."

Callie stepped forward, pulling the ribbon from her pocket.

Her mother's ribbon.

She tied it to the lowest branch, her hands shaking only slightly.

"Hi, Mum," she whispered.

"Sorry this year's a little... crowded."

A soft breeze answered.

Or maybe memory.

She stepped back.

Jax watched her, eyes sharp but softened at the edges.

"Good job," he murmured.

She nodded.

"Now what?"

"Now," Logan said quietly, "we wait."

And they did.

Five minutes.

Seven.

Nine.

Maya's voice spoke in their ears.

"All feeds clean. South path empty. West hedge clear. Bridge shows no movement."

Callie let out a breath she didn't know she was holding.

"Maybe we're early," she said.

"No," Jax said softly. "He's here."

She turned sharply.

"How do you know?"

"Because someone who's watched you this long wouldn't miss this day."

She wanted to argue.

Then she saw Jax's expression.

Not fear.

Not anger.

A hunter recognising another hunter in the dark.

Her pulse picked up.

"Where?" she whispered.

Jax scanned the tree line, his eyes narrowing.

"Close," he murmured. "Too close."

Logan stiffened.

Maya's voice crackled urgently.

"Movement. North side. Someone just stepped off the path—Callie, don't turn around—"

Callie froze.

Her breath stilled.

Jax moved subtly, shifting one foot forward, posture casual but coiled like wire.

"Where exactly?" he asked.

"Five metres behind Callie," Maya said, voice tight.

"Shadow in the hedge. He's watching her. Not moving. Just staring."

Callie's stomach dropped.

She didn't turn.

Couldn't turn.

Jax's voice was low, precise, lethal.

"Callie..."

"Yes?"

"On my count," he whispered,

"you're going to walk toward me."

Her heart hammered.

"Will he follow?"

Jax's jaw clenched.

"Oh," he said softly.

"He's already following."

18

CHAPTER 18 — THE MAN IN THE SHADE

Crimson Creek Memorial Garden
  9:23 a.m.

Maya's voice whispered through the comms like a warning carried on the wind.

"He's right behind her. Five metres. Maybe four."

Callie didn't turn.

Couldn't.

Her heartbeat banged against her ribs hard enough that she felt it in her teeth.

Every instinct screamed: *run.*

But Jax was in front of her, eyes locked onto hers, steady as stone.

"Callie," he said softly,

"walk toward me."

She lifted one foot.

Behind her, gravel shifted.

Logan's voice dropped into a low rumble.

"Target's pacing. Small steps. Tracking her."

Callie took another step.

Her spine prickled—she could *feel* eyes on her, drilling into her back, hungry and possessive.

The air thickened.

The garden seemed to hold its breath.

Jax took one slow step toward her, never breaking eye contact.

"Good. Just like that."

Callie swallowed. "Is he—?"

"Yes," Jax murmured.

"He's coming."

Maya's voice sharpened.

"He's closing distance. Three metres. He's lifting something—"

Callie froze.

Jax's voice cut like a blade.

"Don't stop."

She forced herself forward, knees shaking.

Two metres behind.

One and a half.

She could hear breathing now.

A man's breathing.

Just behind her left ear.

Low.

Too calm.

Callie's vision swam.

Jax's gaze hardened.

"Now," he whispered.

Callie took a final step—

A voice spoke behind her.

Soft.

Almost tender.

"Callie."

Her stomach dropped.

She knew that voice.

It wasn't Evan.

It wasn't anyone from her past.

It was someone... ordinary.

Someone who'd smiled at her in the bakery.

Someone who held doors open.

Someone who fixed a loose latch on her back gate once without being asked.

Noah Briggs.

✦ ✦ ✦

She turned.

Slowly.

Noah stood half-emerged from a gap in the hedges, sunlight catching his face in pieces through the leaves.

Under normal circumstances, he looked harmless—boyish, kind, almost shy.

Today?

His eyes were wrong.

Wide.

Glass-flat.

Lit from inside with something that wasn't admiration.

Obsession.

"Hi, Cal," he whispered, smiling faintly.

"You came. I knew you'd come."

Her body shook.

"Noah... what are you doing here?"

He stepped forward, hands loose at his sides.

"I remembered what today was. Important dates matter. People forget that. But *I* don't."

Jax slid one foot forward, subtle but protective.

"Noah. Stop right there."

Noah's smile twitched.

"You again," he said, voice thinning.

"Always stepping between us."

Callie's breath hitched.

"Noah, there is no 'us.'"

He blinked.

Several times.

Like he was trying to process words that didn't fit his script.

"That's not true," he whispered.

"I've been looking after you. Watching over you. You don't see it, but that's okay. I don't need you to understand everything yet."

Jax's voice dropped to lethal calm.

"Noah. Back away from her."

Noah didn't even look at him.

"Callie, I know I scared you last night. I didn't mean to. I just... I miss when you're alone. It's easier to talk to you then."

Callie felt faint.

Jax shifted, ready to move.

"Noah," he said, steady but steel-hard, "drop what's in your hand."

Callie looked.

Noah held nothing obvious—just a small book.

A notebook.

The same kind of notebook they'd found in the boxes.

She felt the blood drain from her face.

"Noah," she whispered. "What is that?"

He held it out as if offering a gift.

"I wrote something for you. For today. I actually wrote it months ago, but... I didn't know if you'd be ready."

Callie backed up instinctively.

Jax took her place.

"You're not giving her anything," he said.

Noah's face hardened.

"You need to move," he said softly, almost sadly.

"You always ruin the moments. You walk between us and pretend she belongs somewhere else."

Jax didn't blink.

"She belongs *where she chooses*. And right now, she's choosing distance."

A twitch ran through Noah's jaw.

"No," he whispered.

"She's forgotten. She just needs a reminder."

Logan's voice cracked through comms.

"Jax, we have two uniforms in position. On your word—"

"Stand by," Jax murmured.

Callie's hands shook.

Her eyes stung.

"Noah," she said, voice trembling, "you have to listen to me. This isn't healthy. This isn't real—"

"It *is* real!" he snapped.

Birds scattered from the trees.

Callie flinched.

Noah's expression twisted—hurt, angry, desperate.

"I've been here for you since the day you first opened that café!" he shouted.

"I fixed your door when you didn't even know it was broken! I watched over your shop at night! I left notes to let you know you weren't alone—"

Callie gasped.

Jax's eyes flashed with something cold and dangerous.

"You left the note?" he asked quietly.

Noah nodded, chest rising fast.

"You weren't looking at me anymore, Cal. I needed you to see me again."

Maya's whisper over comms was razor-thin:

"Not Evan. Not a ghost. Someone she saw every day."

Logan's voice followed:

"That's our boy. Take him."

Jax didn't look away from Noah.

"No sudden movements. No reaching. Put the notebook down."

Noah's hands trembled.

"Why are you all so scared?" he whispered, confused.

"I'm doing this for her. I'm helping her remember what we are."

Callie's voice broke.

"Noah... there is no 'we.' There never was."

He stared at her.

The hurt in his face cracked into rage so sharp it looked like pain.

"You don't get to say that," he said through clenched teeth.

"You don't get to erase me. I've been here. I've always been here. You just—"

He reached for her.

Fast.

Too fast.

Jax moved before Callie even registered the motion.

One hand grabbed Noah's wrist.

The other slammed Noah to the ground in a controlled, brutal takedown.

Logan was on him in a heartbeat, cuffs flashing silver in the sunlight.

Noah thrashed once, wild, shouting:

"CALLIE! CALLIE, LOOK AT ME! YOU'RE MINE—!"

"Get him up," Jax snapped, voice thunder.

Logan hauled Noah to his feet, pinning him.

Two uniforms rushed in and took control, reading rights while Noah panted and twisted, eyes still locked on Callie.

"Callie," he begged hoarsely.

"Don't let them take me. Please. Please—"

Jax stepped between them, blocking Noah's view.

"That's enough."

Noah strained.

"She needs me! She needs me! You don't know her—"

"I know her," Jax said coldly.

"But you never did."

Noah's face contorted.

A sob.

A snarl.

A tremor of disbelief.

Then he broke.

"I did this for her," he whispered.

"You did this for yourself," Jax said.

The officers dragged him away.

The garden fell quiet except for the distant echo of Noah's cries dissolving down the path.

Callie collapsed to her knees.

Jax caught her before she hit the ground.

"Hey. Hey—Callie. Look at me."

She sobbed once—a raw, shaking sound torn from somewhere deep.

"It was Noah," she whispered.

"Someone I said hi to every morning. Someone I trusted. He was—he was right behind me—"

"I know," Jax murmured, pulling her into his chest.

"I know. I've got you."

She clung to him like gravity itself was failing.

"It was Noah," she said again, voice breaking.

"And I didn't see him at all."

Jax held her tighter, jaw against her temple.

"That's because it wasn't your job to see him," he whispered.

"It was ours."

"And we did."

She cried into him until the trembling eased.

For a long time they stayed like that—Callie breaking in small, exhausted pieces and Jax holding every one.

Finally she whispered,

"Is it over?"

Jax hesitated.

Callie froze.

"What?" she whispered.

Jax met her eyes.

"There were three notebooks in the boxes," he said gently.

"We only brought back two."

Callie's blood ran cold.

"Where's the third?" she breathed.

Jax's voice was low.

"We think someone else took it before we got there."

Her heart stuttered painfully.

"You mean... Noah wasn't working alone?"

Jax didn't look away.

"We're not done yet," he said quietly.

"And neither is he."

19

CHAPTER 19 — THE MISSING NOTEBOOK

Pegasus Mill — Afternoon

Callie sat wrapped in a blanket on the couch, a mug of tea going cold in her hands. Her eyes were rimmed red, exhaustion blurring the edges of everything. She'd stopped shaking an hour ago, but her body hadn't quite accepted safety yet.

Jax stood a few feet away, arms crossed, posture tense — the kind of tense that meant he was replaying every second, measuring every misstep, every mercy.

Logan paced near the whiteboard, running on pure adrenaline.

Chase sat with headphones on, scrubbing every second of audio from the memorial garden.

Maya typed nonstop, eyes flicking across three monitors.

The team was moving, but differently.

Less frantic.

More surgical.

Noah Briggs was in custody.

But the real threat had just stepped out of the shadows.

Callie sipped her tea, barely tasting it.

"So," she said, voice thin, "Someone else was in that house."

Maya nodded. "Yeah."

"And they took one of the notebooks."

"Yeah."

"And that person... what, left it for us to find?"

Jax shook his head. "No. They took it because they didn't want us to see what was in it."

Logan's voice cut in.

"Which means the missing notebook is the most important one."

Callie tightened her grip around the mug. "What could be in it?"

Jax stepped closer.

"A timeline," he said. "A plan. Maybe someone Noah idolised. Someone who shaped his thinking."

Callie looked up sharply.

"You think someone else manipulated him?"

"I think," Jax said carefully, "someone visited him. Someone encouraged him. Someone who knew exactly how to feed an obsession."

Callie blinked.

"That means someone else has been watching me too."

Silence fell.

Not shocked silence.

Confirmed silence.

Jax crouched in front of her, voice softer.

"We never thought Noah acted alone. His movements were too clean. Too precise. He didn't have the confidence for that level of staging."

She swallowed.

"Then... who did?"

"We're going to find out," Jax said.

"We're not stopping."

Logan rubbed his forehead. "We've been going over the timeline from last night. Noah was outside the café, but that ash message on the wall? That wasn't his handwriting."

Callie's stomach dropped.

"How do you know?"

Maya turned her monitor.

Two samples on the screen: Noah's thin, slanted script...

and the ash message — broad, heavy strokes, controlled pressure.

"They're completely different," Maya said. "Different grip strength, different rhythm, different slant. The guy who wrote the ash message is deliberate. Older. More confident."

"More practiced," Jax added.

A cold wave crawled through Callie.

"And the photograph taken from the roof?"

Chase spoke without lifting his eyes.

"Not Noah. Timing doesn't match. He couldn't have left the alley fast enough to reach that vantage point. Someone else was up there."

Callie's breathing hitched.

"So there were two men watching me last night."

Maya corrected gently.

"There were **at least** two."

Callie went rigid.

"At least?"

Maya turned in her chair.

"Noah wasn't the one who bought the red marker. That transaction happened while he was at work."

Chase looked up. "And someone else logged onto the public library computer the same day Noah's first printed photo was produced."

Callie stared at them.

"You're telling me Noah's obsession... was part of someone else's plan?"

"That's exactly what we're telling you," Jax said.

Callie put her hand to her mouth.

"I thought... I thought capturing Noah meant I could breathe again."

Jax shook his head slowly.

"No. Catching Noah means we know what we're up against now."

Her eyes shimmered with fear.

"Which is?"

Jax looked at Logan.

Logan looked at Maya.

Maya looked at Chase.

Then Jax turned back to Callie.

"A shadow stalker," he said quietly.

"Someone who lets others get close first."

An hour later, the Mill had shifted into a different mode — forensic, expansive, hunting something that wasn't careless or desperate but patient.

Maya pulled up a new file.

"We found something in Noah's pocket," she said.

"A receipt."

Callie frowned. "For what?"

"Flowers," Logan said.

"For your mother's memorial."

Callie blinked.

"But Noah didn't bring flowers today."

"Exactly," Maya said.

"Because he didn't buy them."

Chase slid a photo across the table.

Yellowed receipt.

$34.95.

A florist logo.

Handwritten note:

Paid for by friend.

Pick up Friday.

Callie stared.

"What friend?"

Maya zoomed in on the security camera still.

A hooded figure stood at the counter.

Blurred.

Face hidden.

But the posture —

straight back, shoulders even, hands calm, controlled —

was wrong for Noah.

Callie felt the hairs on her arms rise.

Jax leaned forward.

"Freeze it there," he said.

Chase paused the frame.

Someone hovered behind Noah in the video.

Not touching him.

Just close.

Like a shadow.

Maya said quietly:

"The florist said Noah didn't speak. The other man did."

Callie whispered,

"What did he say?"

Maya lifted a small notebook.

"He told them Noah was shy and needed the flowers for a 'special day.' He paid with cash. He gave a false name."

"Which was?" Logan asked.

"Evan Ward."

A shudder ran through Callie.

"But Evan didn't do that," she whispered.

"No," Maya said.

"He didn't."

Callie lifted her eyes slowly.

"Someone used Evan's name.

Why?"

Jax answered first.

"To confuse us.

To point us in the wrong direction.

To hide behind someone else."

Callie's pulse pounded.

"Who would do that?"

Jax's voice softened.

"Someone who knows the town.

Someone who knows your history.

Someone who's been close enough to learn your patterns... but careful enough not to be seen."

Callie shook her head.

"No one fits that. No one—"

Then she froze.

Her breath stopped.

One name.

One possibility.

One face she hadn't seen in years.

Jax saw it the moment she did.

"Callie..." he said carefully.

"Who are you thinking?"

She whispered the name, throat tight.

A name she never thought she'd say again.

A name that had lived in her nightmares long before Noah Briggs ever watched her from a hedge.

"Liam."

Jax went still.

"Your ex?" he asked quietly.

She nodded.

"He was possessive. Controlling. He always knew where I went. Who I saw. He hated that my mother liked you."

Jax's eyes darkened.

"Callie... Liam left town years ago."

Callie shook once.

"What if he came back?" she whispered.

"What if he never left at all?"

The room froze.

Jax stood slowly, something deadly settling into his posture.

"Then," he said quietly,
"we're hunting the wrong man."

20

CHAPTER 20 — THE RED HOUSE

Pegasus Mill — Nightfall

The storm had rolled back over Crimson Creek with a low, electric rumble, as if the sky itself wanted to listen. The Mill glowed in amber light—monitors, maps, evidence boards, and the hum of a team trying to pull truth from shadows.

Callie sat at the central desk, the missing notebook photograph in front of her like a wound. She stared at it until the edges blurred.

One notebook gone.

One ghost still moving.

One name she never thought she'd speak again.

Liam.

Jax paced slow, steady, measured — the way men did when they were trying not to punch the nearest wall in half.

"Callie," he said quietly, "I need you to tell me everything about him."

She swallowed hard.

"I thought he'd changed," she said. "When we started dating, he was... charming. Too charming. The kind of charming that sits wrong in your stomach but looks perfect to everyone else."

Logan lifted a brow. "That tracks."

Callie's voice thinned.

"He started small. Checking my phone. Saying my mum didn't like him. Telling me you were a bad influence."

Jax's jaw tightened.

"He hated you," she added softly.

"He was jealous of you before we ever—"

Her voice broke.

Jax finished for her.

"Before I left."

She nodded, tears stinging.

"When Mum died and I was broken... he liked it. He liked being the one I leaned on. He liked that I stopped going out. Stopped smiling. Stopped fighting him."

Maya sat forward. Logan stilled. Chase's hands paused mid-air over his keyboard.

Callie's eyes were wet, but her voice sharpened.

"When he realised he could control me? It wasn't enough. He wanted to *own* me."

Jax leaned in, every muscle pulled tight.

"What did he do, Callie?"

Her breath trembled.

"He told me he'd wait for me. Even if I moved. Even if I tried to forget him. He said, 'You'll always be mine. Don't make me prove it.'"

The room chilled.

"He left," she said. "One day he was gone. Everyone thought he'd moved north. I didn't question it. I was relieved."

Jax's voice dropped to a dangerous low.

"Callie... do you think he ever left Crimson Creek?"

She stared blankly at the desk.

"I don't know," she whispered.

"But someone knew my routines. Someone knew Mum's memorial. Someone used Evan's name. Someone who knew how to stay invisible."

Chase, quiet until now, said softly:

"And someone who enjoyed letting Noah take the fall."

✦ ✦ ✦

The lights flickered once.

Then the Mill went silent.

Generator.

Monitors.

Radio.

Dead.

A soft click echoed from the far corner of the building — the sound of a breaker tripping by hand.

Jax reached for his weapon instantly.

"Callie behind me," he said, low, controlled.

Maya grabbed a torch. Logan moved to the back entrance. Chase tapped the comms unit — no signal.

"Whole grid's cut," Chase whispered. "Not a blackout. A kill-switch."

A shadow crossed the skylight.

Then a soft, deliberate tapping began.

Tap.

Tap.

Pause.

Tap tap.

Callie froze.

"That's—"

Her voice broke.

She clutched the desk to stay upright.

"That's the sound he used to make when he wanted me to answer the door."

Jax's blood went cold.

"Logan — take the south entrance. Maya — left flank. Chase — lights as fast as you can."

The tapping came again.

Tap.

Pause.

Tap tap tap.

A pattern.

A message.

Callie whispered, "He's saying *Come out*."

Jax stepped closer to her, his presence a wall.

"No one is going anywhere."

Another tap — this one closer. Inside the walls.

Logan's voice crackled softly through his radio.

"Jax... you need to see this."

Jax moved to the rear door, keeping Callie behind him until Maya took her hand. Logan pointed to the back of the Mill.

A Polaroid sat on the concrete.

Fresh.

Still developing.

Jax crouched.

Callie remained frozen, unable to breathe.

Jax turned the photo over slowly, knowing — *knowing* — the world was about to tilt.

White static cleared.

Shapes formed.

Callie gasped.

Maya swore.

Chase whispered, "No..."

Jax's voice came out low, lethal.

"Callie. Look at me. Not the photo."

But she did.

And she collapsed against the doorframe.

Because the Polaroid wasn't of her.

It wasn't of the café.

It wasn't of Noah Briggs.

It was a photo of a house.

A two-storey Queenslander on the edge of Crimson Creek.

Painted red once — now faded to rust.

A house with a sagging verandah.

A house with overgrown palms.

A house she had prayed she'd never see again.

Jax whispered:

"Callie... whose house is that?"

Her lips trembled.

The answer dragged out of her like a broken breath.

"...Liam's."

✦ ✦ ✦

Logan lifted the Polaroid, squinting.

"There's writing on the back."

Jax took it carefully, jaw tight enough to crack.

Two words in thick black marker:

I'M HOME.

Callie clamped her hand over her mouth.

Jax breathed once — slow, deadly — then he stood.

"Get the generator back," he said.

"Get comms up."

"Get Crowe on standby."

Then, quieter, colder:

"Logan. Maya. Chase."

They snapped to attention.

Jax pointed to the photo.

"We're going hunting."

He turned to Callie, voice soft, steady, absolute.

"You're not facing him alone again. Not ever."

Thunder rolled across Crimson Creek like a war drum.

Callie whispered,

"Jax... he knows where we are."

"He knows where *I* am," Jax corrected.

"And he wants me to come to him."

153

He holstered his weapon, eyes like steel.

"Good," he said.

"I was hoping for that."

21

CHAPTER 21 — THE RED HOUSE APPROACH

Crimson Creek — Night
Pegasus Mill

Rain returned in a thin, relentless sheet — the kind that didn't fall so much as cling.

The Mill hummed back to life under Chase's hands, generators coughing awake, monitors flickering from black to blue.

Callie sat on the edge of the workbench, hands trembling hard enough that the mug she tried to hold rattled.

Jax stood in front of her.

Not touching her.

But close enough that she could feel his heat.

"Callie," he said softly. "Look at me."

She did.

Barely.

His voice dropped into something low, anchored, unshakeable.

"We don't go to him because he calls.

We go because *we* decide."

Her breath caught.

"He left the photo because he wants attention," Jax continued. "He wants fear. He wants the narrative."

Logan muttered from the doorway, "He wants a bullet."

Maya elbowed him without looking up from the data feed.

Chase held up a schematic of the property. "No electricity. No neighbours close enough to see or hear anything. Trees along the back fence. Overgrown garden. One way in, two ways out, if you don't count the bush behind it."

Jax nodded once — the soldier fully engaged now.

"Logan, you're with me on entry. Maya, you take perimeter. Chase, you handle comms and motion."

Callie swallowed. "And me?"

Jax turned.

Something in his expression softened — just for her.

"You stay here."

She flinched.

"Jax—"

"No," he said, firmer. "He wants you close. He wants your reaction. He wants the past. You stay in the Mill."

Her voice broke.

"I can't just sit here again—"

"And you won't," Maya said gently, stepping in. "You'll be on comms with me. You'll hear everything."

Callie looked up at Jax again.

His eyes held something raw, fierce, terrifyingly human.

"Callie," he said quietly. "I can't hunt him if I'm worried about you."

Her knees almost gave.

Logan stepped over and put a hand on her shoulder.

"You being safe *is* the mission, Red Wolf."

The nickname cracked her composure.

Her breath shook; she pressed her palms to her eyes.

"He lived there," she whispered. "That house... I used to walk past it every day. He'd stand on the verandah stairs and watch me leave school."

Jax froze.

"You never told me that."

"I didn't think it mattered," she said, voice breaking. "We were kids. He didn't seem—he wasn't—he just—"

Her throat closed.

Jax cupped her face with both hands — gently, but firmly enough that she couldn't look anywhere else.

"You hear me," he whispered.

"What he was then doesn't matter. What he is now does."

Her breath trembled against his palms.

"And now," he said, "he is a threat.

A coward.

A man who thinks fear is power."

The words shook her to her bones.

"Jax..."

He leaned in just enough that she felt his forehead brush hers.

"He's wrong," he whispered.

"You're not alone anymore."

For a moment the room stilled.

The storm, the lights, the monitors — all of it fell quiet.

Callie's eyes closed.

Her breath steadied.

Then she whispered the words that finally unlocked Jax's last restraint.

"Please don't leave me."

His breath hitched.

"I won't," he said. "Not tonight. Not ever again."

Logan cleared his throat loudly from across the room.

"Alright. Lovers' interlude over. Victory waits."

Maya: "Logan."

Logan: "I'm just saying."

Chase: "We don't get paid enough for this."

✦ ✦ ✦

The ute cut through the wet dark, headlights slicing over slick bitumen as Jax drove like a man with purpose — not speed; purpose.

Logan rode shotgun, loading gear, checking mags, cracking his knuckles like he was itching to break something.

"You good?" Logan asked.

"No," Jax said plainly.

"I'm furious."

"Good," Logan replied, leaning back. "Use it."

Jax didn't answer.

His jaw was locked tight.

His knuckles white around the steering wheel.

Every muscle coiled — not with panic, but with decision.

"You think he'll be there?" Logan asked calmly.

Jax didn't blink.

"He left a message," he said.

"He wants an audience. He'll be watching."

"And if he runs?"

Jax's voice dropped to a dangerous low.

"He won't."

Logan smirked. "You sound confident."

"I'm not confident," Jax said.

"I'm done being patient."

Outside, lightning forked across the sky, illuminating the dense line of trees that framed the road. Rain hammered the windshield, bright and violent.

Logan lifted his radio.

"Team One approaching Sundown Road. Eyes open."

Maya's voice crackled through.

"Perimeter drone is up. No heat signatures yet. House looks empty... but I don't trust empty."

Chase added, "Motion sensors are picking up something in the backyard. Could be a possum. Could be a very badly-behaved human."

Jax tightened his grip.

"Stay sharp," he said. "He wants us guessing."

The ute rolled to a slow crawl as the Red House came into view.

Even in the dark, it was unmistakable.

Peeling paint.

Collapsed gutter.

Palm fronds clawing across the verandah like fingers.

The house looked abandoned.

But Jax didn't buy that for a second.

He killed the engine.

Silence hit the ute like a physical blow.

Logan slid out first, weapon drawn.

Jax stepped out into the rain, lifting his face just long enough to taste the storm.

He wasn't afraid.

He wasn't uncertain.

He was ready.

He tapped his radio once.

"Maya. Chase. Positions."

"Perimeter locked," Maya said.

"Motion steady," Chase replied. "One anomaly near the back fence. Could be nothing."

"Copy."

Jax stepped toward the path.

Then he saw it.

A single object placed in the centre of the walkway.

Deliberate.

Waiting.

A **red scarf**.

Callie's scarf.

The same one she wore every winter for years.

The one he remembered helping her wrap around her neck the night her mother died.

Jax crouched slowly.

Logan whispered, "Oh, that's personal."

Jax's voice dropped to a quiet, lethal rumble.

"He's playing with her memories."

"He's playing with *you*," Logan corrected.

Jax's jaw flexed.

"Not for long."

He lifted the scarf. Rain soaked through it instantly — but Jax could still smell her perfume clinging to the fibres.

Lightning flashed behind the Red House.

A silhouette flickered for a fraction of a second behind the curtains.

Logan hissed, "Movement. Second window."

Maya's voice burst over comms:

"Jax, hold—thermal just picked something up inside the living room."

Chase: "Two shapes. Could be reflections. Could be—wait—no. One shape now. One's moved."

Logan raised his weapon.

Jax didn't.

He held the scarf instead.

Then he whispered — low, deadly, personal.

"I'm coming for you."

The house didn't answer.

But the curtain swayed once.

As if someone had just stepped away from the window.

22

CHAPTER 22 — THE BREACH

Sundown Road — The Red House
Night

The storm hadn't just returned — it had thickened, pressing wet heat into the air, sharpening every sound until even the rain felt like surveillance.

The Red House sat hunched behind its palm trees, paint peeling like old scar tissue.

A porch light flickered — not on electricity.

On a battery.

On purpose.

Jax slid the scarf into his jacket, every movement steady, deliberate, controlled in a way that made Logan mutter:

"Oh yeah. He's about to murder someone."

Jax didn't look back.

He lifted his radio.

"Maya. Perimeter."

"All clear. No heat beyond the house. But whatever moved inside is staying in shadows."

"Chase?"

"Comms stable. Motion sensors picking up intermittent spikes near the hallway."

"Copy."

Jax stepped onto the gravel path.

Logan mirrored him, flanking left.

Weapons ready.

Breaths steady.

The house watched them.

It **felt** like watching — the way abandoned places do when they're not actually abandoned.

Jax reached the verandah steps.

One creaked under his weight.

Logan whispered, "He wants us to hear that."

"I know."

Jax knocked once.

Because it was polite.

Because it was controlled.

Because he wanted Liam to understand something very clearly:

This is a hunt.

But *Jax* is the one dictating the pace.

The knock echoed.

Then faded.

Nothing moved.

Jax tested the handle.

Unlocked.

Too easy.

Logan mouthed, *trap.*

Jax gave a single nod.

"On three," he whispered.

"One."

"Two."

" — "

A soft voice spoke through the door.

Not amplified.

Not disguised.

A man's voice.
Quiet.
Almost warm.

"I've been waiting for you, Jax."

Logan stiffened.
Maya whispered, "Holy hell..." through comms.
Jax's hand tightened on the doorframe.
He didn't let it show.
He spoke calmly, evenly.

"Open the door."

A soft chuckle answered.

"That's not how this works."

Logan's fist clenched.
Jax ignored him.
His voice dropped to steel.

"Callie isn't yours."

Silence.
Then:

"She was mine long *before she was yours."*

Callie's voice burst through comms, unsteady:
"Jax—don't react—he wants you angry—"
Jax inhaled once.
Then:

163

"You don't get to say her name."

A soft sigh.

> *"You always thought you were protecting her.*
> *Even when you left her behind."*

Jax's pulse ticked hard in his ears.
Logan muttered, "He's trying to break him. Don't let him, mate."
Jax didn't.
Instead, he said:

> *"She survived you. She won't survive me letting you walk away."*

Another quiet laugh.

> *"You talk like a soldier.*
> *But you bleed like a boy."*

Jax's eyes went cold.

> *"Open. The. Door."*

Nothing.
Then—
CLICK.
The deadbolt slid back on its own.
Logan mouthed *Do not enter.*
Jax entered anyway.

✦ ✦ ✦

The door creaked open, revealing darkness layered in dust and quiet.

The smell hit first — old damp, rotted timber, and something chemical underneath.

The kind of smell that lives in rooms where people plan things they shouldn't.

The hallway stretched long, narrow, lit only by a flickering lantern placed on the floor.

Not electricity.

Not accidental.

A breadcrumb.

Logan swept left.

Jax swept right.

"Clear," Logan murmured.

Jax advanced.

Rain hammered the roof.

Floorboards groaned.

Somewhere deeper inside — a door clicked shut.

Jax froze.

Maya murmured through comms, "Heat signature moving to the back room. Slow. Almost pacing."

Logan whispered, "He knows we're here."

Jax whispered back:

"He wants us deeper."

The hallway walls were lined with photos.

Not framed.

Pinned.

Hundreds.

Callie walking to school.

Callie locking the café.

Callie laughing with a customer.

Callie reading.

Callie crying at her mother's grave.

Logan breathed out a low curse.

"Mate... this is obsessive even by criminal standards."

Jax stared at one photo in particular — Callie sleeping at her workbench two years ago, hair tied back, cheek pressed to her arm.

That photo was taken from inside her café.

He felt something burn low in his chest — not rage.

Conviction.

Logan whispered, "He's been planning this for years."

"Decades," Jax corrected.

He moved forward.

A soft clatter echoed from the kitchen.

Then Liam's voice drifted through the house, warm and conversational:

> *"You never understood, Jax.*
>   *You walked away.*
>   *I didn't."*

Jax stopped.

> *"She was lost. And I found her.*
>   *You left her with nothing."*

Jax's voice was ice.

> *"She told me what you did."*

A soft laugh.

> *"She told you what she* thinks *she remembers.*
>   *Trauma is such a slippery thing."*

Jax stepped forward.

The temperature dropped.
Not physically — emotionally.
Something shifted.

"Do you know why she cried for you?" Liam asked.
"Do you know why she fell apart when you left?"

Jax's teeth clenched.

"Because she thought she wasn't worth staying for."

Jax's vision went white around the edges.
Logan whispered, "Jax. Focus."
Jax did.
He spoke softly.

"You're done talking."
"Am I?" Liam said.
"Because I don't think Callie's done listening."

Callie's breath caught through comms.
"Jax," she whispered, voice broken.
"It's him. It's really him. I know that voice."
Jax's body went still.
Every muscle.
Every thought.
Still.
"Callie," he whispered, "don't listen to him."
But it was too late.
Liam spoke again — not to Jax.

"Calliope."

She sobbed.

Liam chuckled.

"See? She remembers."

Jax snapped.

He surged forward — but Logan caught his shoulder.

"Jax, STOP—he wants you separated."

Jax froze.

Breathing hard.

Liam's voice drifted again:

"Come find me.
  You're close."

A door clicked deeper inside.

Then footsteps retreated.

Slow.

Measured.

Inviting.

Jax whispered:

"We finish this now."

Logan nodded once.

"Together."

Jax lifted his weapon.

Chase murmured, "Motion spike—he's heading to the back room—possibly the basement entrance—"

Maya added, "Thermal's gone—he cut the heat source—he's playing with sensors—"

Then Callie's voice cut through everything:

"Jax—

he doesn't want you to catch him.

He wants you to *follow* him."

Jax's answer was quiet.

Deadly.

"I know."

23

CHAPTER 23 — THE BASEMENT DOOR

Sundown Road — The Red House
Night

The hallway narrowed, the walls crowding closer with every step Jax took.

Logan followed at his shoulder — steady, silent, eyes sharp.

The storm pounded the roof like a fist.

A door at the end of the hallway stood half-open.

Light pooled under it.

Not steady light — flickering.

Like a candle.

Jax lifted his radio.

"Maya. Thermal?"

Static.

Then—

"Jax... the whole house just dropped offline. Sensors gone. Cameras gone. He's jamming the frequency."

Chase cut in, tense:

"I can't regain visual. He's using outdated scramblers. Old-school. He knew exactly what tech we'd bring."

Logan muttered, "Smart bastard."

Jax didn't respond.

His hand hovered over the doorknob.

He wasn't afraid.

Fear was too simple.

What he felt was colder:

Recognition.

This wasn't a random stalker.

This wasn't an opportunist.

This was someone who had spent years studying Callie.

Years watching Jax.

Years planning the exact moment the past would finally catch the present.

Jax turned the knob slowly.

Callie's voice cracked through comms — trembling, frantic:

"Jax—wait—don't go in alone—"

Logan squeezed Jax's shoulder.

"I'm right here."

Jax pushed the door open.

✦ ✦ ✦

The room was empty.

A single lantern burned on the floor.

Above it, photographs hung in a tight, deliberate circle — dozens of Polaroids, pinned with thumbtacks.

Callie laughing.

Callie tying her apron.

Callie hugging her mum outside the hospice.

Jax's spine went rigid.

He stepped closer.

Logan whispered, "Mate... these weren't taken from a distance. Half of these are inside angles."

Jax already knew.

And then he saw it.

In the centre of the photo circle —

A picture of Callie sleeping at the Mill.

Taken hours ago.

Under it, handwritten:

YOU STILL CAN'T PROTECT HER.

Logan breathed out hard.

"Oh, that's it. I'm done playing nice."

Jax didn't move.

Callie's voice whispered through the speakers — he heard her breath catch.

"Is that... my mum's scarf on the floor?"

Jax's heart slammed once against his ribs.

He hadn't noticed it before.

A second scarf.

Grey.

Frayed at the ends.

Her mother's hospice scarf.

Folded carefully on the tiles.

Logan whispered, "He's recreating things."

"No," Jax said softly.

"He's weaponising them."

Callie choked over comms.

"Jax... please... get out of there..."

He moved toward the photographs anyway.

He couldn't stop himself.

Every instinct screamed danger —

but something deeper screamed truth.

He brushed the centre photo aside.

Behind it, a small latch glinted.

A hidden door.

A basement entrance.

Logan exhaled. "Oh, that's bad."

Jax's hand tightened around the latch.

Callie's voice shredded.

"Jax, don't—please don't—"

He paused.

Just long enough to say, quietly:

"I'm ending this."

He pulled the hatch open.

◆ ◆ ◆

The smell hit first.

Not rot.

Not decay.

Something worse:

Old disinfectant.

Dust.

And the faint trace of perfume Callie used three years ago.

Jax went still.

Logan's skin prickled.

"Oh no," Logan whispered. "He didn't—tell me he didn't—"

Jax descended the first step.

The staircase groaned, old and damp.

Callie whispered through comms, voice paper-thin:

"That basement... that's where he'd disappear for hours. He said he was fixing things. He never let me go down there. Not once."

Jax gripped his radio.

"Callie.

Listen to me.

You weren't the reason he hid things."

Callie sobbed, "I think I was."

Jax stopped.

Right there on the stairs.

His voice lowered into something fierce enough to shake the air:

"He hid this because he knew I'd find it one day.

Not you."

Silence.

Then Callie's broken reply:

"You left.

He didn't."

The words pierced Jax deeper than any blade.

He whispered, not to her, not to Logan—

To himself.

"And I will never make that mistake again."

He stepped deeper.

✦ ✦ ✦

The basement opened into a narrow chamber lit only by another lantern.

The walls were covered.

Covered.

Floor to ceiling.

Not with photos — but with handwritten pages.

Dozens.

Hundreds.

Pinned in neat lines.

Jax scanned one near the door.

His stomach turned.

Not threats.

Not rants.

Letters.

Unsaved drafts.

Never sent.

Every one addressed to the same name:

CALLIOPE.

Logan whispered, "Jesus Christ... he's been writing to her for years."

Jax read another.

Then another.

Letters about seeing her walk by.

Letters about watching her close the café.

Letters about Jax.

Logan read over his shoulder.

"He calls you the obstacle.

He calls himself the balance.

He thinks he's—oh hell—he thinks he's the one who can *fix* her."

Jax's jaw tightened so hard it hurt.

Callie's breath trembled over comms.

"That handwriting... that's... that's his."

Jax inhaled.

And then he saw it.

The final page.

Pinned dead centre.

Different handwriting.

Not Liam's.

Shakier.

Older.

Jax's blood ran cold.

Logan lifted the paper slowly.

"Jax," he whispered.

"You need to see this."

Jax took it.

Read it.

And the world stopped.

The note said:

"You left her alone.

So I kept her safe.

You should thank me.

—L."

Jax froze.

"Why... why is that not Liam's handwriting?" Logan whispered.

Jax shook his head slowly.

Because it wasn't.

Because Jax recognised it.

He had seen that handwriting before.

Callie whispered, terrified:

"Jax... what is it...?"

Jax didn't speak.

He couldn't.

Because the handwriting on the note wasn't Liam's.

It was familiar.

Painfully, intimately familiar.

It was Evan Ward's.

Logan whispered, "Oh no. No. No. Tell me this isn't a double act."

Jax stared at the page.

Evan.

Liam.

One disappeared.

One stayed.

Or—

One was the visible shadow.

The other was the real one.

Jax lifted the radio.

His voice was calm.

Too calm.

"Maya," he said.

"Call Chase.

Seal the perimeter.

And lock down Crimson Creek."

Callie whispered, "Jax... who wrote it?"

He closed his eyes.

Opened them again.

And said the words that shattered her world:

"It wasn't Liam down here."

Callie's breath cracked.

"What?"

Jax stepped back from the wall.

"It was Evan."

Logan swore under his breath.

Callie's voice broke into a sob.

"No—no—Evan—Evan was harmless—Evan was—he would never—"

Jax spoke softly.

Painfully.

"Callie...

he's been in love with you since you were fourteen.

You never saw him because he was designed to be unseen."

Silence clamped the basement.

Then—

From the shadows behind the furnace—

A soft, deliberate whisper drifted out:

"She noticed me."

Jax spun — weapon raised.

Logan snapped his rifle into place.

But the shadows remained shadows.

No shape.

No movement.

Only a voice.

A voice Callie knew.

A voice she trusted.

A voice she never feared.

Until now.

"I kept her safe while you ran."

Jax's blood iced.

"I promised her mother I'd watch over her."

Jax froze.

Logan whispered, "That's... that's not possible..."

Jax swallowed once.

Hard.

And whispered back:

"He knew her mother."

24

CHAPTER 24 — THE MAN IN THE DOORWAY

Crimson Creek — The Basement
Night

The shadows swallowed the corners of the room.

The lantern flickered against the walls of handwritten obsession.

Jax held his gun steady, but his pulse thundered in his ears.

Logan circled wide, rifle up, breath controlled.

The voice drifted again from behind the furnace — soft, familiar, unbearably calm.

"She noticed me before any of you did."

Callie's whisper cracked through comms:

"Jax... is that really... Evan?"

Jax exhaled once, eyes locked on the darkness.

"Callie," he said softly, "tell me the truth. Did he ever meet your mother?"

A long silence.

Then—

"I... I don't know. She had visitors from the book club, from the hospice group... he lived two streets over but—"

The voice interrupted her, gentle and warm.

"I brought her soup when she was sick."

Callie's breath snapped.

"No... no, that was Mrs. Tanner—"

"She wasn't home that day. So I left it for her."

Jax whispered, "Callie... think."

Her voice trembled into memory.

"I... remember Mum saying an angel left soup once. She laughed about it. She said she didn't have the strength to thank them..."

Another beat.

"...but she said they must've been watching over her."

The voice softened.

"She was right."

Logan muttered, "Christ almighty, he's not a stalker. He's a ghost with keys."

Jax took a slow step forward.

"Evan. Come out where I can see you."

Silence.

Then—

"She needed someone to stay after her mother died. You left. I didn't."

Jax's eyes went flint-hard.

"That's not staying," he said quietly. "That's *waiting*."

The lantern flickered.

Footsteps whispered.

And then he stepped out.

Evan Ward stood in the half-light.

Not sweating.

Not trembling.

Not wild-eyed.

Just... present.

Present in the way someone is when they're finally done pretending.

His hair was damp from rain.

His shirt was buttoned neatly — too neatly.

His posture calm, hands relaxed at his sides.

A man who believed he was safe here.

A man who believed he belonged here.

Jax's finger hovered by the trigger.

Logan breathed, "Don't twitch, mate. He's not reading the room like a normal offender."

Evan smiled faintly.

Not cruel.

Not gloating.

Content.

"You made her cry this morning, Jax."

The basement froze.

Jax's voice dropped low.

"How would you know that?"

"I saw her leave the cabin. Her eyes were swollen. You held her too tight."

Jax's skin crawled.

He hadn't noticed anything watching them.

Nothing.

No vehicle.

No drone.

No person.

Logan whispered, "He walked the bushland. On foot. No electronics. That's why we didn't ping him."

Evan's smile widened, almost shy.

"I don't need technology. I know her routines. Her footsteps. Her breathing."

Callie sobbed through comms.

"Evan... why?"

He looked up, eyes soft.

"Because she asked me to."

Jax snarled, "She never asked for you."

Evan tilted his head, as if explaining something simple to a child.

"Not in words."

✦ ✦ ✦

Jax tightened his grip. "Callie. Listen carefully. When did your mum meet him?"

Callie's breath came shallow.

"During her last year... she was lonely. She'd stopped going out. Some neighbour checked in sometimes—"

Evan lifted a hand gently.

"Not some neighbour. Me."

Callie whispered, horrified, "Mum would've told me."

"She didn't," Evan said softly, "because she didn't want you to worry. She knew you were fragile then. You'd lost so much. She told me you needed space to grow."

Callie whispered, "You're lying."
He smiled sadly.

"Your mother gave me the house key."

Everything stopped.
Logan swore under his breath.
"Oh, bloody hell—no—Cal—"
Callie's voice shattered.
"Mum didn't—did NOT—she wouldn't have—"

"She left it under the blue pot," Evan continued. "She told me where it was. She asked me to help her with the heating when she was too tired. She asked me to stay while she slept."

Jax's hand twitched on the gun.
This wasn't just possession.
This wasn't just obsession.
This was a **delusion built from truth.**
Callie whispered, broken:
"She was sick. She was trusting anyone who brought tea and kept the lights steady. She didn't—she didn't understand—"

"She understood perfectly," Evan said quietly. "She told me to keep looking after you. She said you'd try to do too much alone. She said you'd push people away."

Callie pressed both hands to her mouth.

"No... no... Mum wouldn't have tied me to someone—"

Evan stepped closer, hands still calm.

"She didn't tie you to me. She asked me to watch you. Just until you stopped breaking."

Jax finally spoke.

He didn't shout.

He didn't tremble.

He *cut*.

"Your mother didn't mean *follow her daughter into her shower*.

She didn't mean *sleep in her bloody hallway*.

She didn't mean *copy her boyfriend's walk*."

Evan blinked slowly.

"You left."

Jax's jaw clenched.

"That isn't an answer."

"It's the only answer," Evan murmured. *"She cried when you left her, Jax. I heard her."*

Jax stiffened.

Logan whispered, "Oh hell—he was in the house that night."

Evan nodded, almost proud.

"I was downstairs. I heard everything."

Jax's breathing stalled.

He remembered that night like a wound:

Callie sobbing in the hallway.

Her begging him not to go.
Her voice breaking.
Evan had been there.
Listening.
Listening and learning.
Jax whispered, "You listened to her heartbreak like it was a lesson."
Evan smiled.

"Exactly."

✦ ✦ ✦

The air changed.
Jax saw it —
Logan saw it —
the shift in Evan's posture.
His shoulders loosened.
His head lowered.
His voice deepened with something colder.

"You think you know what she needs.
But I've watched her longer than you've loved her."

Jax's finger found the guard of his trigger.
Logan murmured, "We're out of time."
Evan took one slow step back toward the shadows.

"She's calling for me. She always has."

Jax growled, "She's terrified of you."

"She's terrified of losing me."

Logan muttered, "Delusion level ten. We need to take him before he escalates."

Evan tilted his head.

Then his smile disappeared.

Completely.

"I'm going to her now."

He turned.

Jax fired.

The bullet struck the concrete right beside Evan's foot — deliberate, a warning line drawn with steel.

"Take one more step," Jax said through gritted teeth,

"and you don't walk anywhere again."

Evan paused.

Just paused.

Then whispered:

"You won't shoot me.
  She wouldn't forgive you."

Jax's breathing went razor sharp.

"Try me."

Another beat.

Evan smiled again — that soft, unsettling smile.

"Then let's see who she runs to first."

And before Logan could lunge

  before Jax could fire

  before Maya could trace—

Evan slipped into the darkness behind the furnace and vanished.

✦ ✦ ✦

The silence that followed was deafening.

Jax ran the last steps, sweeping the dark, but Evan was gone.

Gone like smoke.

Logan cursed loudly.

"Son of a—he had a second exit. Bastard built a tunnel."

Jax hit the comm, voice raw:

"Maya—lock down the whole bloody block. Evan Ward is active. He is delusional. He had access to Callie's house years ago. He's been watching everything."

Maya's sharp inhale cut the channel.

"What? Jax—Evan is at the café right now. On camera. He just walked up to the door."

Jax froze.

"No."

Callie gasped.

"No—no—Jax—Jax he can't—"

Maya's voice grew frantic.

"He's knocking. Repeatedly. His hands are shaking. Jax—he's—he's calling for her. He's saying her name."

Callie's breath shredded.

"Jax—please—"

Jax sprinted for the stairs.

Logan right behind him.

"Move move move—"

Jax didn't respond.

He was already gone.

Running harder than he ever had in his life.

25

CHAPTER 25 — THE DOOR HE SHOULD NEVER HAVE TOUCHED

Crimson Creek — Red Wolf Books & Brew
Night

The café windows glowed gold against the storm-dark street, a small oasis of light in a town that suddenly felt too quiet.

Inside, Callie paced behind the counter, phone in hand, breath unsteady.

Maya's voice crackled over comms:

"He's still at the door... he's not trying to break in... he's just *knocking.* Slow. Rhythmic. As if he's expecting you to open."

Callie pressed a hand to her stomach, nausea curling tight.

"Jax—how far?"

Jax didn't answer—not with words.

She heard him instead.

The *boots.*

The gravel.

The sprint.

He was running harder than she'd ever heard him run.

Logan's voice cut through the line, sharp and breathless:

"Two minutes out. Keep her behind the counter."

Chase added, "Camera angle confirms: Evan's smiling at the glass. Like she's just late to let him in."

Callie's heartbeat spiked.

"I can't—he can't—Jax, please—"

Maya interrupted gently, "He won't reach you, Callie. Not tonight. Not ever again."

Callie's eyes flicked to the front door.

Evan's silhouette pressed lightly against the glass—head bowed, breath misting the pane.

He knocked once more.

Soft.

Tapping the rhythm of her mother's old lullaby.

Her blood went ice-cold.

"That's my mum's—"

She choked on the rest.

Maya whispered, horrified:

"He learned it from her. God, he used *everything*."

Callie stumbled back, hand gripping the edge of the counter.

That was the moment she saw—

He wasn't holding flowers.

He wasn't holding a note.

He was holding her mother's scarf.

Her mother's hospice scarf.

The grey one she'd lost years ago.

Her knees nearly buckled.

"He took it," she whispered. "He took it from her room. He took it and—"

Maya's voice sharpened:

"Jax is seconds away. Stay low."

Jax rounded the corner of the alley, lungs burning, boots skidding through rainwater.

He saw the silhouette at the café door.

Saw the scarf.

Saw the way Evan leaned forward, pressing his forehead to the glass as if whispering a prayer.

Jax didn't think.

Didn't breathe.

He roared:

"EVAN! Step away from the door RIGHT NOW."

Evan froze.

Then turned.

Slowly.

Calmly.

A gentle smile forming—

not for Jax—

but for the idea of Callie hearing him.

> *"She called me."*

Jax's jaw clenched so tight it hurt.

"She didn't call you. She doesn't WANT you. Step back."

Evan shook his head, rain streaking his hair.

> *"You don't understand. Her mother entrusted her to me. She entrusted her heart."*

Jax stepped forward, stance low and lethal.

"The only person Callie trusts with her heart is inside the café."

Evan blinked.

Confused.

Slow.

Like a child being told a rule that didn't make sense.

> *"...She told me I was the one who stayed."*

Logan arrived behind Jax, panting.

Maya's car slid to a stop at the curb.

Logan raised his weapon. "Don't make me use this, mate."

But Evan didn't look at Logan.

He only looked at Jax.

And said something that made every muscle in Jax's body coil tight:

> *"You left her once.*
> *You will leave again.*
> *But I won't."*

Jax's voice dropped into that terrifying quiet he only used before violence.

"Callie is not yours."

Evan took one step closer to the glass.

One hand lifted.

One fingertip touched Callie's name on the painted sign.

> *"She always was."*

Jax moved.

Fast.

Too fast for Evan to react.

He slammed him back from the door, one arm across Evan's chest, pinning him to the café brickwork. The scarf dropped from Evan's hand onto the wet pavement.

Logan flanked him instantly, wrist restraints ready.

Evan didn't fight.

He just stared at Jax with an unsettling calm.

> *"She'll forgive me before she forgives you."*

That did it.

Jax's face went cold and sharp.

"You don't know a single damn thing about her."

Evan smiled.

"It's adorable you believe that."

Logan snapped the cuffs around his wrists.

"You're done, friend."

Evan looked past them to the café window.

To Callie's shadow behind the counter.

His smile softened.

> *"She's scared.*
> *I'll go to her.*
> *She needs me to explain."*

Jax stepped in front of him, blocking his view.

"You will never go near her again.

You will never speak to her again.

You will never breathe her name again."

Evan tilted his head, studying him.

> *"You're shaking.*
> *That means you're afraid of losing her."*

Jax didn't blink.

"I'm shaking because I'm deciding how gentle I need to be to get you in the back of that police car."

Logan muttered, "For the record, I vote *not very.*"

Sirens grew louder—two patrol cars approaching from the bridge.

Evan's calm cracked.

Just a hair.

He whispered:

> *"Don't take me away from her.*
> *She needs someone who won't abandon her."*

Jax leaned close.

"You stalked her. You broke into her home. You stole from her dying mother. You watched her sleep. You terrorised her."

Evan blinked slowly, as if trying to process the words.

"I kept her safe."

The sirens pulled up. Doors slammed. Officers ran toward them.

Evan twisted once—just once—panic breaking through delusion.

"I HAVE TO SEE HER—"

Jax slammed him flat against the brickwork before he could lunge.

"She doesn't want to see you."

Evan's breath shuddered.

He whispered, broken—

"But she's mine."

Jax's voice was steel and fire:

"Not anymore."

The officers took him.

Evan didn't fight—

he just kept looking toward the café window.

Toward Callie's silhouette.

As if waiting for her to stop them.

She didn't.

She stood still.

Trembling.

Watching everything.

Watching him finally be removed from her life like a blade pulled from a wound.

✦ ✦ ✦

Callie stood behind the counter, hands shaking so hard the spoon in her grip rattled against the metal bench.

The door opened softly.

Rain gusted in.

Jax stepped inside, soaked, chest rising and falling with leftover adrenaline.

She looked at him.

And then—

She broke.

Collapsed into him so fast he barely caught her.

Her sob hit his shoulder first.

Then her shaking.

Then her fists gripping the back of his shirt like she was terrified he would dissolve.

He wrapped both arms around her, holding her steady, holding her tight, holding her *together*.

"It's over," he murmured into her hair.

"It's over, Callie. I've got you. I've got you."

Her voice cracked like glass.

"He had Mum's scarf—

he knew her—

he... he saw me cry—

Jax I can't—

I can't breathe—"

He cupped her head gently, grounding her to his chest.

"You're safe.

He'll never touch you again.

I swear it."

She gripped him harder.

"I thought I was going crazy. I thought I imagined the footsteps. I thought—I thought I was the one losing control—"

"You weren't," he said fiercely. "He was."

"I trusted him. I *trusted* him—"

"You did nothing wrong."

Her crying softened, breaths still uneven but no longer spiralling.

She whispered into his shirt:

"I don't want him in my head anymore."

Jax pressed his lips to the top of her hair.

"Then let me stay there instead."

She lifted her face.

Her eyes were wet.

Her lips trembled.

But her voice was steady when she answered:

"Yes."

He kissed her.

Not gently.

Not cautiously.

But with the fierce, overwhelming relief of two people finally free of the shadow that's been following them.

The storm outside broke into rain.

The danger was done.

The healing had begun.

26

CHAPTER 26 — AFTER THE FALL

Red Wolf Books & Brew
Night

The sirens faded sooner than Callie expected.

As if the whole town had agreed it was time to let silence return.

The café lights glowed warm against the storm-dark windows.

Rain dripped steadily down the glass, streaking the sign, smudging the reflection of the chalkboard and the empty tables.

Jax sat with her on the back steps, both of them damp from rain, adrenaline slowly burning out of their bloodstreams.

Callie's head rested against his shoulder.

His arm wrapped around her like muscle memory.

They didn't speak for a long time.

The world felt suspended—quiet, heavy, safe in a way Callie couldn't quite understand yet.

Finally, she whispered:

"Why didn't I see it?"

Jax's thumb brushed the back of her hand.

"Because you had no reason to suspect him."

"I trusted him."

"You trusted humanity," he corrected softly. "A decent trait. A brave one.

Don't let him turn that into something you hate."

She stared at the rain pooling along the brick path.

"I keep thinking about Mum.

What she would've wanted...

what she would say now..."

He angled toward her, gentle but firm.

"She'd say exactly what I'm saying: this wasn't your fault."

Callie let out a small, unsteady laugh.

"You're very sure of that."

"Because it's true," he said. "Because you were grieving. She was sick. People come and go in moments like that. You don't interrogate every kindness. You shouldn't have had to."

Her throat tightened.

"Then why do I feel like I let him in?"

Jax touched her cheek—thumb light, careful over the butterfly tape.

"Because he was patient.

And clever.

And because he hid behind the kind of man he pretended to be."

She swallowed.

"I still feel stupid."

"You're not," he said sharply. "You were targeted."

She looked up.

He wasn't angry at her.

He was angry for her.

Angry enough to shake.

Angry enough to bleed.

And for the first time...

she saw what it cost him to keep that anger contained.

She turned her hand and laced her fingers through his.

"Jax... did you think I'd hate you?"

He didn't look at her.

The quiet answer slipped out anyway.

"Yes."

A breath caught in her lungs.

"Why?"

"Because I left you once. And I was terrified you'd see tonight as proof I failed again."

She shifted, sliding her legs across his lap, cupping his jaw with both hands.

"Hey," she whispered, leaning her forehead against his. "Look at me."

He did.

Barely.

"You didn't fail me," she said. "Not then. And definitely not now."

His breath shook.

Not much.

But enough.

"You're here," she said. "And I am still here. You didn't lose me."

He exhaled, long and low, and his hands found her waist like the truth finally had somewhere to land.

"You matter to me," he said. "More than I ever admitted. More than I should've let happen."

"And I matter to myself," she said, voice steadier than she felt. "More than he ever understood."

She brushed her knuckles along his temple, soft.

"Do you understand?" she asked.

Jax's answer was a quiet, reverent:

"Yes."

✦ ✦ ✦

The back door opened without a knock.

Logan stepped in first, dripping rain and smelling like a man who had run through hell and back. Maya followed, hair plastered to her forehead, Chase behind her, carrying a toolkit and looking exhausted.

They paused when they saw Callie sitting on Jax's lap, wrapped in his arms.

Logan's grin ghosted at the corners of his mouth.

"Well," he said softly, "looks like you two are alive."

Callie wiped her cheeks with the heel of her hand.

"Barely."

Maya crouched in front of her.

"You did everything right," she said. "You listened. You stayed put. You let us do our job. You didn't freeze."

Callie swallowed. "I felt like I froze."

Maya shook her head.

"You survived."

Logan nudged Jax with his boot.

"You good?"

"Not yet," Jax said, fingers still locked around Callie's waist. "But I will be."

Chase opened a first-aid kit without being asked.

"You're both scraped up. And your shoulder's bleeding through that stupid black shirt again, Jax."

Jax didn't move.

Callie slid off his lap gently.

"I'll clean it," she said.

Jax started to object.

She lifted one eyebrow.

"Let me take care of you."

He quieted immediately.

Logan, walking past, muttered to Maya, "That's it. They're done for."

Maya smirked. "Took long enough."

✦ ✦ ✦

The café closed early.

The storm softened.

Pegasus remained—

in chairs, in corners, sprawled on countertops—

like they weren't going anywhere until the last tremor faded.

Callie sat on the counter, swinging her feet.

199

Jax sat on a milk crate in front of her while she cleaned the scrape along his shoulder.

He winced once.

She smiled faintly. "Big baby."

"Knife grazed me. You try it."

"Didn't you get stabbed for a living?"

"Different context."

She dabbed the wound gently, fingers brushing his skin.

For the first time all night, Jax's rigid posture loosened.

He let her care for him.

Let himself be still.

"You're shaking," she whispered.

"I almost lost you."

"You didn't."

"Not the point."

She leaned down, kissed his forehead.

"Jax... I'm not going anywhere."

He looked up at her with something so raw and open it almost hurt to see.

"Promise me."

"I promise."

The café hummed with the sound of Pegasus repacking gear.

The rain softened to a whisper on the roof.

Jax rested his palm over her knee.

"We're going to make a new routine," he said softly. "One he never touched."

She nodded.

"I want that."

He rose, cupped her face gently, kissed her—soft at first, then deeper, grounding, a promise more than a question.

When they separated, she whispered:

"Stay tonight?"

He smiled, small and honest.

"I'm not leaving."

"Good," she said. "Neither am I."

✦ ✦ ✦

At midnight, Pegasus said their goodnights.

Maya squeezed Callie's hand.

Logan locked the door behind him without asking.

Chase gave an awkward half-hug, mumbling something about system logs.

And then it was just Jax and Callie.

The café dimmed to a single lamp.

Her head found his chest.

His chin rested on her hair.

Their breathing synced.

Not passion.

Not adrenaline.

Something quieter.

Something that finally felt like theirs.

"You know what I want tomorrow?" Callie whispered.

"What?"

"Normal."

Jax kissed the crown of her head.

"Then we'll build it."

She smiled into his shirt.

"Together."

He held her tighter.

"Always."

27

CHAPTER 27 — STATEMENT

Crimson Creek Police Station
  Mid-Morning

The station smelled like old carpet, wet jackets, and photocopier toner.

Callie sat at the edge of the hard plastic chair, fingers linked tightly in her lap, the fluorescent lights turning her skin pale.

Jax sat beside her, knee brushing hers just enough to anchor her.

Logan stood against the far wall, arms crossed.

Maya flipped through her tablet, eyes sharp.

Chase paced the hallway outside, refusing to go further because the last time he'd entered an interview room he'd accidentally tripped over a constable's chair.

Callie breathed slowly.

In and out.

She was here by choice — a fact she kept reminding herself every thirty seconds.

Jax touched her hand, only the slightest pressure.

"You okay?" he murmured.

"No," she whispered. "But I'm doing it anyway."

His lips softened. "That's the definition of brave."

Before she could respond, the door opened.

Detective Sergeant Hall stepped in — mid-50s, weathered face, neat moustache, the resigned expression of a man who had seen far too much of other people's darkness. He placed a folder on the metal table.

"Callie Hart?"

She nodded.

"Thanks for coming in. Pegasus has briefed us, but I need your version on record."

He paused. "I know this is difficult."

Callie's throat tightened.

Jax's thumb stroked the side of her hand — slow, grounding.

"I can do it," she said.

Hall clicked his pen.

"Start from the beginning. In your own words."

Callie inhaled.

"My mother died three years ago."

She hadn't expected to start there.

The sentence cracked something open — sharp, painful, but honest.

Hall nodded. "Take your time."

"She was home for most of her last year. Hospice care. Neighbours came and went. Friends visited. I didn't know everyone who brought flowers or meals."

Her fingers curled.

"I didn't know Evan was one of them."

Jax's jaw tightened.

Hall wrote quickly. "And after her passing?"

"He... found ways to stay connected without me realising."

"Such as?"

"He'd leave little things. A bag of lemons when the café first opened. A card with no name. A magazine Mum used to read."

Her voice shook. "I thought they were coincidences."

Hall's eyebrows lifted a fraction.

"Then I moved here. To Crimson Creek."

"The notes started?"

203

"Yes," she whispered. "Short ones first. Harmless, I thought. Compliments. Then... possessive things. Someone watching me close the café. Someone knowing my routine."

She swallowed hard. "Someone calling me 'Calliope.' Only Mum called me that."

Silence folded around the room.

Logan shifted, visibly restraining his temper.

Hall tapped the pen once.

"And recently?"

Callie looked at the table.

"He broke into my flat. He left a brick through the Mill window. He... followed me. He wrote things on walls. He knew what songs my mother sang. He..."

She trembled.

"He took her scarf."

Jax slid his hand up her spine, steady and warm.

Hall spoke gently. "And last night?"

"He came to the café door."

Her eyes glazed.

"He knocked the rhythm of my mother's lullaby. He said my name. He... smiled."

Her whole body shivered.

Jax's hand tightened over hers, grounding her again.

He didn't speak.

He didn't need to.

Hall nodded slowly.

"That's enough for today."

But Callie lifted her chin.

"No," she said quietly. "It isn't."

She processed breath through trembling lips.

"I want his name on every page of that report. I want a restraining order that actually restrains. I want every camera in this town on high alert. I want the judge to know what he did."

She swallowed hard.

"I want to say the parts I've been too ashamed to say out loud."

Hall stilled. "Go on."

Callie closed her eyes.

"He watched me sleep."

Jax inhaled sharply.

"He stood outside my bedroom door once," she whispered. "I thought it was a dream. I even told myself afterward I imagined it. But... I didn't."

The room froze.

Maya's stylus hovered mid-air.

Logan cursed under his breath.

Jax's face carved itself into something lethal.

But Callie kept going.

"He mirrored Jax. The clothes. The walk. The tone. I thought it was nostalgia when I missed Jax."

She looked at Jax, tears rising.

"It wasn't nostalgia. It was him."

Jax's jaw trembled just once — barely — then his hand came up to cradle the back of her neck.

"Callie..."

She pressed her forehead to his for a second, steadying.

Then she turned back to Hall.

"And I want you to know: I'm not afraid of him anymore."

Her voice strengthened.

"I'm angry."

Hall finally allowed a flicker of respect.

"That," he said, "will hold up in court better than fear."

✦ ✦ ✦

Hall left to file the statement.

Maya packed up quietly, giving Callie space.

Logan leaned against the wall, rubbing the back of his neck.

Callie sat still.

Then —

Her breath broke.

She didn't cry loudly.

It wasn't a sobbing collapse.

It was a release.

A letting go of pressure she had carried for three years.

Jax moved before she even lifted her head.

He knelt in front of her chair, hands warm on her knees.

"I'm here," he whispered.

She nodded.

"I know."

"You did the hardest part. You told the truth."

"It hurts."

"It's supposed to," he murmured. "Truth is heavy. But now you're not carrying it alone."

Her fingers curled into his shirt.

"I can breathe again," she whispered.

He smiled softly.

"That's the point."

Logan opened the door quietly, keeping watch.

Maya leaned in.

"You want to head back to the Mill? I can get the kettle going before you get there."

Callie wiped her cheeks with her sleeve.

"Yes," she said. "But... I want one thing first."

"What's that?" Jax asked.

She stood.

Stepped into him.

Wrapped her arms around his waist.

Held him tight — not from fear, not from need, but from choice.

And whispered into his chest:

"Thank you for coming back."

Jax exhaled shakily, arms wrapping around her in a fierce, unguarded hold.

"I'm never leaving again."

"Good," she whispered. "Because I don't want to run anymore."

✦ ✦ ✦

They stepped into the sunlight together.

Rain had washed the streets.

The breeze felt new.

Light felt different — clearer, sharper, like the world had reset.

Callie looked up at him.

"What happens now?"

Jax brushed a wet curl from her cheek.

"Now?"

He smiled.

"Now we live."

She threaded her fingers through his.

"Together?"

"Always," he said softly.

Logan shouted from the ute, "Either kiss or get in the car, you two!"

Maya rolled her eyes. "Ignore him. He hasn't slept."

Chase honked the horn. "I AM THE DESIGNATED SUPPORTIVE FRIEND."

Callie laughed — the first real, unbroken laugh since the café attack.

She kissed Jax's cheek, then tugged him toward the ute.

"Take me home," she murmured.

"Anywhere you want," he answered.

And for the first time in her adult life— she believed him.

28

CHAPTER 28 — RED WOLF, RECLAIMED

Crimson Creek — Late Afternoon

Red Wolf Books & Brew still smelled faintly of rain and adrenaline.

The morning's chaos had settled into something calmer — the hush after a storm where the world feels strangely new.

Callie unlocked the café door with a slow, steady breath.

The bell chimed.

A small sound.

But today it sounded like victory.

Jax followed behind her, carrying a toolbox that wasn't his.

Chase had shoved it into his hands earlier with a proud, "Fix something. It's good therapy."

Logan carried a mop.

He didn't know why.

He just felt it looked symbolic.

Maya held three takeaway coffees and a bag of muffins because, in her experience, trauma recovery required baked goods.

Callie stepped into the centre of the café.

Her café.

Her space.

Her voice came small but sure:

"I want my place to feel like mine again."

Jax set down the toolbox and nodded.

"Then we'll make it so."

They didn't need instructions.

Pegasus moved like a unit.

Jax checked the frames on the windows, reinforcing the weak points.

Logan took down the cracked chalkboard and rewrote the menu in his awful handwriting (no one had the heart to tell him).

Chase replaced the backdoor lightbulb and then felt like a hero.

Maya re-organised the supply shelves because she found them "psychologically upsetting."

Callie mopped the floor, humming softly.

She felt safe.

A strange sensation after so long.

Jax noticed.

He straightened from the front windows and leaned against the frame, arms folded, watching her with a look that wasn't intense—but was absolutely full.

"You're humming," he said.

She paused.

"Oh. Sorry—"

"Don't be sorry," he said softly. "It's good. It means you're coming back to yourself."

Her chest warmed.

"Honestly, I feel like I'm coming back to... a better version of myself."

He stepped closer.

"How so?"

"Because I'm not pretending anymore," she said, meeting his eyes. "Not pretending I'm fine. Not pretending I'm not scared. Not pretending I don't want..."

She slowed.

"...more."

His breath caught.

"And what does 'more' mean to you?"

She held his gaze.

"You."

It hit him like a physical thing.

Not lust.

Not desperation.

Something deeper.

Something that hit straight to where he'd been guarding himself for years.

He exhaled, long and slow.

"Callie..."

But she shook her head gently.

"You don't have to say anything yet. I just need you to know I'm not afraid to say it now."

He stepped close enough to brush her cheek with the back of his fingers.

"I heard you," he murmured.

"I really heard you."

She smiled.

And then Maya walked past carrying a stack of teacups and muttered, "God, you two radiate enough emotional tension to power a small city," before disappearing into the storeroom.

Callie covered her face with both hands.

Jax laughed.

A real laugh.

Low and warm.

✦ ✦ ✦

Callie found it in a drawer beneath the counter — the scarf Evan had dropped in the rain, folded neatly by Maya earlier so Callie didn't have to see it the moment she walked in.

She held it gently.

Grey wool.

Faint lavender scent.

Her mother's.

Her throat tightened.

Jax came up beside her.

"You don't have to keep it," he said quietly. "We can burn it. Donate it. Throw it away."

She shook her head slowly.

"No. He doesn't get to take this too. I'll wash it. I'll wear it. It belonged to her. Not to him."

Jax watched her—a look of awe, admiration, something close to reverence.

"You're stronger than you think," he murmured.

"I'm strong because I'm not alone anymore."

Jax's breath hitched.

She didn't see it.

But he felt it.

Every word of it.

✦ ✦ ✦

The team eventually left, giving them space without announcing they were giving them space.

By sunset, it was just Callie and Jax again, sitting on the steps behind the café, a breeze cooling the last of the day's heat.

Callie leaned her head against his shoulder.

"You stayed," she whispered.

"I told you I would."

She brushed her thumb lightly along his hand.

"You sound certain."

"I am."

She shifted, turning slightly to look at him more fully.

"Why?"

Jax's expression softened—

not guarded, not restrained—

open.

"Because somewhere between the nightmares and the silence...
between the old ghosts and the café lights...
I realised I wasn't staying because you needed me."
He reached out, tucking a strand of hair behind her ear.
"I'm staying because *I want you.*
All of you.
The brave parts.
The scared parts.
The parts that survived without me and the parts that want me now."
Her heart stumbled.
Softly.
Dangerously.
"Jax..."
He leaned his forehead to hers.
"Tell me if that's too much."
She cupped his jaw with both hands.
"It's everything I wanted to hear."
They stayed like that, foreheads touching, breaths slow, fingers tangled.
Nothing rushed.
Nothing forced.
Just two people choosing each other in the quiet.
Jax pulled back slightly.
"There's one thing I want us to agree on."
She blinked softly.
"What?"
"No more pretending we're fine when we're not."
She nodded.
"And no more disappearing on each other," he added.
She took a breath.
"Okay," she whispered. "But then... no more leaving without saying goodbye."
His chest tightened.
"I swear it."

"And no more lying about feelings," she said.

He smirked. "Is that aimed at me or you?"

"Both of us."

"Fair."

"And," she added with a small smile, "no more rage-punching walls."

Jax grinned.

"No promises."

She nudged him gently.

He nudged her back.

Soft.

Playful.

New.

And then she leaned her head on his shoulder again.

"Jax?"

"Yeah?"

"Stay with me tonight."

His breath stopped.

But his voice didn't.

"Always."

And for the first time—

Callie believed the night ahead wouldn't be haunted.

It would be hers.

And his.

Together.

29

CHAPTER 29 — NO MORE HIDING

Crimson Creek — The Police Station

Callie had never seen the station this quiet.

No ringing phones.

No raised voices.

No hum of chatter.

Just the steady drone of the air-conditioning and the subtle buzz of fluorescent lights.

Jax walked beside her — not in front of her, not behind her, but beside her, his hand brushing hers just enough to anchor her without taking space she didn't give.

Maya and Logan waited outside the interview room. Chase sat on a bench, quietly dismantling a pen and putting it back together in a way that suggested he was trying not to punch someone.

Callie stopped at the threshold.

"You ready?" Jax asked.

"No," she said honestly.

"But I'm doing it anyway."

His eyes warmed. "That's what courage looks like."

She stepped inside.

✦ ✦ ✦

The interview room was clinical, the table scarred with old pen scrapes. Officer Dana Crowe sat with a thick file in front of her, expression unusually sober.

"Callie," Crowe began. "You understand this is being recorded?"

"I do."

"And you're giving this statement of your own free will?"

"Yes."

Callie's voice didn't shake.

She told the story.

All of it.

The notes.

The photos.

The trespassing.

The camera hidden in her flowers.

The figure watching from across the river.

The way Evan had slid back into her life with a predator's patience, cloaked in nostalgia.

Jax didn't interrupt.

Didn't shift.

Didn't even breathe wrong.

Just sat behind her, chair angled, silent and steady as a mountain.

When Callie finished, Crowe closed the file sharply.

"That's enough for the magistrate to approve an AVO with immediate enforcement."

Callie exhaled slowly.

Not relief.

Not yet.

But permission to breathe.

✦ ✦ ✦

He looked smaller.

That was her first thought.

Evan sat on the edge of the cell cot, hands cuffed loosely in front of him. The buzz of the fluorescent light above cast him in a sickly, stark blue.

When he looked up, his eyes flickered — recognition, guilt, something like longing twisted into something far darker.

"Callie," he breathed. "I was worried about you."

Jax moved forward, but Callie lifted her hand ever so slightly.

"I've got this."

Evan's smile cracked under the weight of her calm.

"You're not well," he said. "You've been paranoid. You always spiraled without me—"

"You watched me sleep," she cut in.

"You filmed my café.

You followed me through town.

You put a camera in my flowers."

Each word was a clean blade.

He swallowed. "I was protecting you."

"That's not protection," she said. "That's obsession."

He pressed his palms together, eyes pleading.

"Callie, you don't understand how much I—"

"No," she said, voice quiet but absolute.

"You don't understand that you don't get to define what loving me looks like."

For the first time since this nightmare began, *his power cracked.*

His shoulders curled inward.

His eyes darted to Jax — who stood unmoving, unreadable.

"You replaced me," Evan whispered.

"That's what this is. He turned you against me."

Callie stepped closer to the bars, voice steady.

"I didn't replace you. I left you. And you never accepted it."

His lip trembled. "I could've fixed it."

"There was nothing to fix," she said. "Because we were over."

He shook his head.

And then his voice dropped to a whisper that chilled the room:

"You're still mine."

Jax stiffened.

Callie didn't flinch.

"No," she said.

"Red Wolf is mine.

My life is mine.

And I will never give you another piece of it."

Crowe hit the buzzer.

Guards moved in.

Evan screamed her name once, raw and furious, but the sound cut clean as the doors slammed.

Callie stood perfectly still.

Jax stepped to her side, voice low.

"You didn't shake."

"I thought I would," she whispered.

"You didn't."

"Does it make me awful that I feel... good?"

He shook his head softly.

"It makes you free."

✦ ✦ ✦

Late afternoon sunlight cut through the courthouse hallway like gold wire. People drifted in and out: farmers, tradies, parents, bored teenagers dragged here for mischief.

Callie sat between Jax and Maya as the clerk called their case.

The magistrate was a severe woman in her mid-fifties with eyes sharp enough to cut lies into ribbons.

"Ms. Hart," the magistrate said. "You've requested an Apprehended Violence Order under section 45. Is that correct?"

"Yes," Callie said.

"Do you fear the respondent?"

Callie breathed in.

She remembered the photo sent at 4:12 AM.

The camera hidden in her planter.

The figure standing by the river.

The note left on her café window.

The time he whispered her name through the vent when she thought she was alone.

"Yes," she said.

"But I'm not afraid to say so anymore."

The magistrate nodded once, satisfied.

"Order granted. Effective immediately."

Callie closed her eyes.

This time it was relief.

Jax's hand brushed hers under the bench, a silent *I'm right here.*

Maya squeezed her shoulder.

Logan whispered, "Told you — breakfast, handcuffs, justice."

She snorted through a tear.

The magistrate tapped her pen.

"This court recognises the bravery of the applicant," she said. "And encourages her to pursue a peaceful life moving forward."

Jax glanced at Callie, something flickering in his expression.

She felt it.

The possibility of peace.

The possibility of a future.

The possibility of him.

✦ ✦ ✦

They stepped into late afternoon sun.

The warmth brushed her face, softer than it had felt in weeks.

Jax stood beside her as the others drifted ahead.

"Callie," he said gently. "You did something many people can't."

"I didn't do it alone."

"No," he said. "But you were the one who stood up and said 'no more.' That matters."

She looked at him, eyes warm, tired, hopeful.

"What now?" she whispered.

"Now," he said, stepping closer, "you get your life back."

She smiled softly.

"And you?"

He brushed a knuckle down her cheek.

"I'm exactly where I want to be."

Her breath hitched.

"Jax..."

He lowered his voice.

"Let me stay. Not because you're afraid... but because you don't have to be anymore."

Her answer was soft, steady, sure:

"Stay."

And he nodded once.

Like a vow.

30

CHAPTER 30 — THE QUIET AFTER

Crimson Creek — Dusk

The sun dipped low over the river, turning the surface to molten gold. The kind of light that made everything look softer than it had any right to. The kind of light Callie had nearly forgotten existed.

Jax unlocked the front door of the refurbished café, stepping back so she could walk in first.

The scent hit her immediately — fresh timber, varnish, ground coffee, faint citrus from the cleaning spray Maya had insisted on using. The smashed window was gone. The word *Mine* scrubbed from existence. The space looked like itself again, only sturdier.

Like her.

She stood very still.

"You okay?" Jax asked quietly.

She nodded.

Then shook her head.

Then nodded again.

Her voice came out a whisper. "It feels like walking back into my own skin."

He didn't touch her — didn't push, didn't crowd — just waited.

Callie stepped deeper into the café, fingertips trailing the fresh varnish on the counter. The place didn't feel haunted anymore. It felt reclaimed.

"I thought the fear would follow me in," she said. "But it didn't."

"That's because it never lived here," Jax said. "He did. And now he doesn't."

She turned toward him, the soft dusk light catching in her eyes.

"Thank you."

"For what?"

"For not leaving," she said. "Not once. Not when I was shaking. Not when I was angry. Not when I didn't know how to breathe."

His expression shifted — something between humility and something deeper he wasn't ready to name.

"Callie... you don't owe me anything."

"No," she said softly. "I don't. But I'm grateful."

He exhaled slowly, shoulders loosening for the first time in days.

And then she asked the question he hadn't expected.

"Are you staying tonight?"

His chest tightened — not with desire, but something far older, far quieter.

"If you want me to," he said.

She stepped closer, brushing a fingertip over the healed scrape on his forearm.

"I'm not asking because I'm scared," she whispered.

"I know."

"I'm asking because I don't want to sit in the silence alone."

He nodded once, slow. "Then I'm here."

Later — in the kitchen behind the café

They made tea the way exhausted people do: without thought, without conversation, letting the small ordinary tasks stitch them back together.

Callie filled the kettle. Jax reached for mugs. Their hands brushed once — a spark, not heat, but recognition.

"Feels like a lifetime since I've done this," she said.

He looked at her, eyes softer than she'd ever seen. "Feels like one for me too."

Steam curled between them, carrying the scent of peppermint and something calmer.

She leaned against the counter. "You know… today wasn't just about him."

"No?"

"It was about me," she said. "About choosing myself. About not being the girl who apologises for surviving."

Jax's jaw flexed — the kind of reaction he didn't allow around most people.

"You were never weak," he said. "You were never anyone's."

"I was afraid."

"That's not the same thing."

She swallowed. "I think I want to learn the difference."

"Then you will," he said simply.

The kettle clicked off. He poured the tea. They sat at the small table tucked near the back wall.

For a long time, they just breathed in the quiet.

The world felt different.

Not fixed.

Not perfect.

But clean.

For the first time in months, Callie wasn't holding herself tight.

For the first time in years, Jax didn't feel like he needed a wall between himself and the world.

"You know what scares me?" Callie said softly.

He lifted his eyes. "Tell me."

"That after all of this… when the quiet finally came back… I'd feel empty."

"And do you?"

She shook her head. "No. I feel… space."

She touched her chest lightly.

"Like there's room now."

He sat forward, elbows on his knees, voice low.

"Callie... you don't have to fill it with anything yet."

Her smile was soft. "It's okay if I fill a little of it with you."

The admission caught him. He didn't move. Didn't reach for her. Just let the words settle in the air between them — fragile, warm, real.

"You sure?" he asked.

"Yes."

He nodded.

And that was all.

No kiss.

No rush.

No pressure.

Just the beginning of something that didn't need to be named yet.

Something that would grow in the spaces fear used to occupy.

✦ ✦ ✦

Later — Jax Walking Her Home

Crimson Creek was quiet. Streetlights blinked on one by one, spilling honeyed pools across the footpath. A couple of locals nodded at them as they passed — subtle, supportive. Word travelled fast here.

Callie walked close but not clinging, arms wrapped around herself more out of comfort than fear.

"You look lighter," Jax said.

"I feel lighter."

He hesitated, then: "I'm proud of you."

Callie stopped walking.

"Say it again."

"I'm proud of you."

Her eyes glistened.

"You know... I didn't realise how much I needed someone to say that."

"You earned it."

She reached out, threading her fingers through his — tentative, gentle, testing.

He didn't flinch.

He didn't tense.

He just held her hand like it was the most natural thing in the world.

They walked the rest of the way like that.

Her front steps waited in the warm gold of the porch light. She turned to him.

"You don't have to stay outside."

"I'm not going anywhere," he said.

And she smiled — a real one, the first in days.

"Good."

She opened the door.

Jax followed her in.

Not as a guard.

Not as a shield.

But as someone she'd chosen.

Someone who'd earned a place in the quiet after.

31

CHAPTER 31 — SHADOWS DON'T GET THE LAST WORD

Crimson Creek — Early Morning

Callie woke before Jax.

Light spilled across her bedroom wall in soft, lazy stripes — the kind of dawn that didn't rush anyone. The kind that suggested the world could wait a moment.

Jax sat in the armchair near the window, long legs stretched out, boots off, shirt loose around his shoulders. He hadn't meant to fall asleep — she could tell by the way his head tilted slightly to one side, the way one hand still rested near the holster strapped to the chair leg.

Old habits refusing to surrender.

She watched him for a full minute.

Not in fear.

Not in need.

Just... noticing.

He looked younger like this. Softer. Human in a way he didn't often allow himself to be.

"You're staring," he murmured without opening his eyes.

She smiled. "You weren't supposed to catch me."

"I did," he said, cracking one eye. "And you don't have to stop."

She threw a pillow at him.

He caught it one-handed, smirking.

"I made coffee," she said.

"Of course you did."

They drank it in silence at her tiny kitchen table, steam curling between them like a truce.

"You sleep at all?" she asked.

"Enough."

"Enough for you," she said. "Not enough for humans."

His mouth tugged upward. "You calling me something else?"

"A stubborn mule," she said, sipping. "With guns."

He huffed a laugh — rare, low, real.

But beneath it, something shifted.

A flicker of tension in his shoulders.

A shadow behind the eyes.

She tilted her head. "What?"

He didn't look at her.

Which meant it was something he didn't want to burden her with.

"Jax."

He inhaled.

"When someone like Evan escalates this far," he said quietly, "there are usually questions from higher up."

"Questions?"

"From Pegasus oversight. From QPS. From people who like reports clean and quiet."

Her stomach dipped, not in fear — but in anger.

"So someone thinks this is your fault?"

"Someone always thinks something."

"And what do you think?"

He finally looked at her.

"I think I'd do it again."

The simplicity of it hit harder than any confession.

"You protected me," she said.

"I stood with you," he corrected. "You protected yourself."

She set her mug down.

"Is this going to cost you something?"

He hesitated.

She read it instantly.

"It is."

"It might."

"I don't want you getting dragged because of me."

He leaned forward, forearms braced on his knees.

"Callie. Look at me."

She did.

"This isn't your fault. And you're not responsible for the choices I make."

"But Pegasus—"

"Pegasus can live with it," he said. "I care about one thing: you're safe."

Her throat tightened.

Not with fear.

With something weightier.

"Jax..."

"Don't worry about me," he said softly. "Not today."

She breathed out slowly.

For the moment, she let it go.

But only for the moment.

✦ ✦ ✦

Later — The Café

The bell above the café door chimed for the first time in days.

Callie froze.

Jax stood.

But it was only Mrs. Penrose from the bakery across the street, carrying a box and wearing the expression of a woman on a mission.

"Heard what happened," the older woman said gruffly. "Didn't like it. Don't like him. Didn't like him when you were dating either."

Callie blinked. "Thank you?"

"Brought danishes," Mrs. Penrose said, thrusting the box toward her. "Sugar helps. Eat."

Callie opened it.

Freshly baked custard swirls glistened inside.

"That's... really kind," she said.

Mrs. Penrose gave Jax a once-over. "You the one who stayed with her?"

"Yes, ma'am."

"You armed?"

"Yes, ma'am."

"Good. Make sure she eats."

And then the woman turned and left, bell chiming cheerfully behind her.

Callie laughed — genuinely, freely.

"She's terrifying."

Jax nodded. "She threatened to hit Logan with a rolling pin once."

"She did?"

"He deserved it."

They ate pastry over the counter, crumbs everywhere, sugar dusting the air.

It felt normal.

It felt healing.

It felt human.

And Callie realised she wasn't flinching at the door anymore.

Not waiting for the next shadow.

Not anticipating the next intrusion.

Jax noticed.

"You're breathing easier," he said.

"Yeah," she whispered. "I am."

"Good," he said.

But something in his tone told her there was still a weight he was carrying. One he wasn't naming yet.

She touched his arm lightly. "Whatever's coming... we'll handle it."

He looked at her, and for a moment the shields he always held up — the humour, the stoicism, the distance — flickered.

"You don't know what's coming," he murmured.

"No," she said softly. "But neither do you."

He exhaled a breath that sounded almost like a surrender.

She didn't push further.

Not yet.

✦ ✦ ✦

Afternoon — Walking Back by the River

They took the long way home — down Old Ferry Road, where the river bent around the trees and caught the afternoon sun in sparkling flecks.

Kids rode scooters.

A couple walked their kelpie.

Life happened quietly.

"Strange," Callie said. "How normal everything looks."

"It usually does," Jax said.

"Even when someone's hunting you."

He nodded. "Especially then."

The wind curled around them.

Callie's voice softened.

"Does it bother you," she asked, "that you let someone get this close?"

Jax didn't answer at first.

Then:

"It bothers me that he got close to you."

She halted.

Turned to him.

Heart open, unafraid.

"And that says everything."

He held her gaze a long moment.

Something settled between them — unspoken, heavy, unmistakable.

Then he said quietly:

"Callie... we're not done."

"With the case?"

"With any of it."

She stepped closer, close enough to feel the warmth radiating from him.

"Then don't run from it."

"I'm not," he said.

"Good," she replied. "Because neither am I."

The river shimmered behind them.

The breeze eased.

And the quiet after didn't feel empty anymore.

It felt like the beginning of a world they might build — brick by brick, choice by choice — once the shadows learned they didn't get the last word.

32

CHAPTER 32 — THE FIRST DAY SHE WASN'T AFRAID

Crimson Creek — Morning Light

The first thing Callie noticed was the light.

Not weak.

Not filtered through fear.

Not the kind she'd learned to brace against.

Just morning light — gold and clean and unapologetic — pouring through her kitchen window like it had always belonged there.

She stood barefoot on the cool tiles, hair messy from sleep, a mug warming both hands. The kettle still clicked softly from the boil. Somewhere behind her, floorboards creaked as Jax stretched awake.

For the first time in what felt like years, her pulse didn't spike at the sound.

She smiled.

Jax's voice was rough with sleep. "You're up early."

"I'm not hiding today," she said, pouring his coffee into a chipped ceramic mug he'd somehow claimed as his.

"You haven't been hiding," he murmured, accepting it. "You've been surviving."

She shrugged. "Surviving still feels like hiding on the inside."

He leaned against the doorframe, hair tousled, shirt hanging loose, the kind of relaxed she'd rarely seen in him. "And today?"

She breathed in, slow.

The air smelled like warm coffee and lemon dish soap and her own life reclaiming itself.

"Today," she said, "I want to be part of the world again."

Something softened in him — a subtle exhale, like the tension he'd held coiled overnight finally eased.

"You deserve that," he said.

✦ ✦ ✦

They didn't drive.

Callie insisted.

"I want to feel the day," she'd said.

So they walked.

The footpath still glistened with yesterday's rain, a faint shimmer on the asphalt catching the new sun. Crimson Creek felt gentler this morning — less sharp, less watchful, as if the whole town sensed a shift inside her.

A couple walking a kelpie waved.

Mr. Morris from the hardware store called out, "Morning, Callie! Heard the café's reopening!"

She returned each greeting with a smile that felt real.

Jax walked beside her, not hovering, not scanning every shadow — though she knew he was still alert. That was his nature. His burden. But he let the edges soften for her.

At the river bend, she stopped.

The water moved slow, catching sunlight in ripples.

"This used to scare me," she said quietly. "Not the river — the idea of being watched while I crossed it."

"Does it now?"

She dipped her head. "No."

And because she wanted to — because she could — she linked her fingers through his.

His thumb brushed the back of her hand.

Not claiming.

Not guarding.

Just... there.

A steady presence that didn't demand anything from her.

They walked on.

✦ ✦ ✦

The Café — Reopening

The bell above the door chimed a soft welcome.

Callie stepped inside and inhaled deeply.

Coffee beans.

Fresh timber.

New beginnings.

"I'd forgotten how good it smells in here," she said.

Jax pulled a stool from under the counter. "I'll stay out of the way."

"You're not in the way."

He blinked, thrown by how casually she said it.

She tied her apron — a motion she hadn't done in days — and flicked the switch on the espresso machine. The hum was familiar, grounding, alive.

"Feels like standing up again," she said as the machine warmed.

"Then stand," Jax answered.

She laughed softly. "Bossy."

"Honest."

He helped where she let him — wiping tables, checking the back door bolt, replacing a light bulb she couldn't reach. But mostly he watched her find herself again.

When she pulled the first shot of the morning, she exhaled a shaky breath.

"Still got it," she whispered.

"You never lost it," he said.

Customers trickled in — Mrs. Penrose for a latte. The crane-operator brothers for flat whites. Teenagers for iced mochas. Everyone gentler than usual, their smiles touched with something like pride.

Callie moved between tables, the first-day nerves turning into something else:

Confidence.

Ownership.

Belonging.

Jax sat at the counter, boots planted, posture casual but eyes soft as he watched her reclaim every inch of her space.

At one point she caught him looking.

He didn't look away.

Neither did she.

✦ ✦ ✦

Afternoon — A Different Silence

By late afternoon the rush had eased. The café was warm, quiet, sun-dappled through the window. Callie sat opposite Jax at a small table, two empty cups between them.

"I didn't freeze once," she said. "Not even when someone walked behind me."

"I noticed."

"And I didn't think about him every time the bell chimed."

"Good."

"And I didn't keep looking over my shoulder."

"Even better."

She nudged his foot with hers under the table. "You're allowed to smile, you know."

"I am smiling."

"That's your *micro-smile*. Not the real one."

He sighed — dramatic, theatrical — earning a quiet laugh from her.

Then he leaned back, face warming into something gentle, unguarded.

"There it is," she whispered. "That's the one."

"You earned it," he said.

The quiet that settled between them wasn't empty anymore.

It was full.

Soft.

Safe.

"You know," she said, "it's strange."

"What is?"

"I keep thinking the world should feel different now that I'm... not afraid."

He watched her closely. "Does it?"

She looked around the café — her café — bathed in the kind of warm afternoon light she once thought she'd never feel again.

"It feels like mine again."

"And you?" he asked quietly. "Do *you* feel like yours again?"

She held his gaze.

"Yeah," she said softly. "I think I do."

Something in him relaxed deeply — something he'd been holding tight even when he said he wasn't.

"Good," he murmured.

"Jax?"

"Mm?"

"I want you here."

He didn't ask what she meant.

He didn't need to.

"I'm not going anywhere," he said.

And this time, she believed him without hesitation.

Because it wasn't fear holding her up now.

It was strength.

Her own.

And him — not as a shield she needed...

...but as a choice she made.

33

CHAPTER 33 — THE NIGHT THE WORLD GOT QUIET

Crimson Creek — After Closing

The café door clicked shut behind the last customer, and the street settled into its evening hush — that soft, slow pulse Crimson Creek had when the day was finally done. Golden light slanted across the floor, warming the timber and catching in the air like dust suspended mid-breath.

Callie flipped the sign to CLOSED, then turned to find Jax wiping down a table that absolutely didn't need wiping.

He looked up.

Caught.

Didn't apologise.

"You okay?" he asked.

"I think I might be," she said — the same simple truth she'd woken with this morning. Except now it felt fuller, steadier.

He set the cloth down and studied her the way only he did — not scanning for threats, but reading her. Checking whether she was standing on solid ground or on shaking earth.

Tonight, she was standing.

Really standing.

"Come home with me," she said quietly. Not rushed. Not shy. Just... certain.

A slow warmth moved through his expression. "Yeah," he said. "Okay."

✦ ✦ ✦

They walked the two blocks to her flat in a dusk washed pink and lavender. Streetlamps blinked awake one by one. A dog barked in the distance. Two teenagers skated past, laughing. Nothing dangerous. Nothing sharp.

For the first time, the silence between them wasn't shaped by fear or tension.

It was shaped by something else—

something warm,

slow,

pulling them closer step by step.

At her building, she unlocked the door and paused—

not afraid,

not bracing—

just letting the moment stretch, breathe, settle.

"You sure?" Jax asked, voice low.

She met his eyes. "I'm sure."

He gave a single nod, quiet, respectful. The kind that said he would follow her pace, not his own.

She stepped inside.

He followed.

✦ ✦ ✦

The air smelled faintly of cinnamon and lemon oil, with a thread of something warm—her. Evening light pooled on the floorboards. The space felt smaller with him in it, but in the way that makes a room feel full, not crowded.

She slipped off her shoes.

He did the same.

237

"Tea?" she asked, lifting the kettle.

"Tea's good," he said.

If someone had told her weeks ago that she'd be making tea for Jax Hart in her kitchen without shaking, she would've laughed. Or cried.

But here she was:

barefoot, calm, alive in her own home.

Steam rose.

The kettle clicked.

She handed him a mug and kept one for herself.

Their fingers brushed.

Neither pulled away.

◆ ◆ ◆

They sat close.

Not touching, but close enough that she could feel the warmth radiate off him.

He held his mug in both hands, elbows on his knees, eyes not on the room but on her.

"You fought for today," he said softly. "You did that."

"I didn't do it alone."

"You did more than you know."

She turned, tucking one leg under herself. "Why are you always like this?"

"Like what?"

"So steady."

"I'm not," he said. "I just look steady when it's about you."

Her breath caught.

Her heart didn't race.

It... expanded.

He set his mug down. Slowly. Like he didn't want to startle the moment.

"Callie," he said, "if this is too fast—"

"It's not."

"If you need space—"

"I need you close."

The air changed — a soft shift, a tether pulling tight.

She reached out first, fingers brushing the back of his hand.

He answered without hesitation, palm sliding against hers, warm and rough.

He didn't lean in.

She did.

And he met her halfway —

slow, deliberate, the kind of kiss that isn't about wanting but about choosing.

Choosing her.

Choosing now.

Choosing the life that waited on this side of fear.

His hand cupped her jaw gently, thumb sweeping across her cheekbone.

Nothing rushed.

Nothing demanding.

Just presence.

Just him.

Just her.

Just quiet.

When they finally pulled back, breath slow, foreheads resting together, she whispered:

"I didn't feel afraid at all."

He smiled—small, soft, the kind that lived in his eyes more than his mouth.

"Good," he murmured. "Because I'm not going anywhere."

She slid closer, resting her head against his shoulder.

His arm lifted.

Settled around her.

Held.

Not protectively.

Not out of duty.

Because he wanted to.

Because she let him.

They stayed like that for a long time, the night stretching around them like a warm blanket, the world outside fading to a hum.

No one watching.

No footsteps.

No notes on glass.

No ghosts.

Just two people who had walked through hell and finally found a place to sit down.

At some point, the room darkened and the lights of the street below traced soft patterns across the ceiling. Her breathing slowed.

"You falling asleep?" he asked, voice a low rumble.

"Thinking."

"About what?"

She shifted closer, fingers curling into the fabric of his shirt. "Tomorrow."

"Yeah?" he murmured, brushing a kiss into her hair. "What about it?"

"That it's ours."

He exhaled—a sound of relief, of hope, of something like joy.

Then he whispered it back, warm against her temple:

"Ours."

The first night the world was quiet.

The first night she wasn't afraid.

The first night he let himself truly stay.

And the night everything ahead of them began.

34

CHAPTER 34— THE NIGHT THEY CAME HOME TO EACH OTHER

Crimson Creek — Late evening

The night air was warm when they stepped into her flat, the kind of warmth that softened the edges of everything — street noise, shadows, breath. Jax closed the door behind them with a quiet click that seemed to settle in Callie's chest like a heartbeat.

Her home looked different tonight.

No fear in the corners.

No threat lurking in the quiet.

Just soft lamplight, the faint trace of cinnamon, and the impossible feeling that the world had tilted back into place.

She slipped off her jacket. He watched her — not hungrily, not with expectation, but with the steady awe of a man seeing someone he'd missed for far too long.

"You look... lighter," he whispered.

"So do you."

He huffed a half-laugh. "Don't think anyone's ever told me that."

"Well," she said, stepping closer, "there's a first time for everything."

Their hands brushed.

It felt like a spark waking a memory.

He swallowed. "Callie, if you're not sure—"

"I am," she said. No hesitation. "But that's not why I asked you here."

He blinked, thrown. "No?"

She shook her head, stepping into his space, her fingertips finding the edge of his shirt.

"I need you to hear something first."

Her voice wasn't trembling —

but her breath was.

He gave her all of his attention. Quiet. Patient. Ready to catch anything she dropped.

"I thought the worst part of everything that happened," she said softly, "was the fear."

Jax's jaw tightened, remorse flickering.

"But it wasn't," she whispered. "It was losing the life I thought I'd have. It was losing myself... and losing you."

His breath left him —

not in pain —

in recognition.

"Callie..."

She touched his chest.

Right over his heartbeat.

Right where he used to tuck her in when the world felt too big.

"You were the first person who ever made me feel safe without telling me to be small."

He closed his eyes — just for a moment — holding back an entire storm.

She kept going, voice breaking and mending in the same breath.

"And when you left, I didn't hate you. I just didn't know how to forgive you for choosing duty over us."

He opened his eyes — raw, blue, unguarded.

"I chose wrong," he said. "I know that. I carried it every day."

"And I carried the empty space," she whispered.

Silence.

Thick.

Electric.

She curled her fingers into the fabric of his shirt, drawing him a breath closer.

"I don't want to carry emptiness anymore."

His control snapped — not into force or hunger but into honesty.

He cupped her face with both hands, voice roughened by everything he'd held back.

"You were never empty, Callie. You were the brightest damn thing in my life. And I walked away because I thought I'd break you."

She shook her head, tears shining.

"You didn't break me. You broke yourself."

A sound escaped him — small, devastated, reverent — and then he kissed her.

Not to claim.

Not to possess.

Not to erase anything.

To answer every word she'd just given him.

Her hands slid up his shoulders, then into his hair, pulling him closer with a soft, aching certainty that stole his breath.

When they broke for air, foreheads touching, she whispered:

"This isn't about fear anymore."

He nodded once, slow.

"This is about us."

"About coming home," she breathed.

The next kiss was deeper — not rushed, not wild —

but sure.

Renewal.

Recognition.

A beginning disguised as a return.

His thumbs traced her cheekbones.

Her fingers slipped along the warm line of his jaw.

Their breathing synced the way it used to —

the way muscle memory remembers long before the mind catches up.

He kissed the corner of her mouth.

Her jaw.

Her shoulder.

Slow, reverent, as if learning her all over again.

She answered with soft sighs and fingertips that drew constellations across his skin.

Heat bloomed — not sudden but inevitable —

the kind that builds from emotion rather than desire alone.

She whispered his name like it meant something sacred.

He whispered hers like he'd been waiting years to say it this soft.

When he lifted her — carefully, gently, giving her every chance to stop him —

she tightened her arms around his shoulders instead.

A yes.

A welcome.

A return.

He carried her to the bedroom, setting her down with a tenderness that made her eyes shine again.

"You're sure?" he murmured.

She touched his face, steady.

"Jax... this is the safest I've felt with anyone in my life."

Something deep inside him cracked open.

Softened.

Settled.

He kissed her again —

slow, warm, unguarded —

and they sank into the moment together, clothes whispering, breath merging, the kind of closeness that didn't need details to be intimate.

The rest happened the way real lovers happen:

mutual, slow, shared, emotional, heated —

felt more than shown.

The room dimmed.

The world fell away.

And two people who had been broken in all the same places finally found the way back into each other's arms.

Fade to instinct.

Fade to warmth.

Fade to home.

35

CHAPTER 35 — MORNING LIKE A PROMISE

Crimson Creek — Early Morning

Callie woke before she opened her eyes.

She felt him first.

His warmth at her back.

His breath — slow, steady — brushing the nape of her neck.

His arm draped over her waist in a way that wasn't possessive, just... certain.

And the gentle weight of his fingers resting exactly where they'd settled in her sleep.

Safe.

Held.

Home.

Her eyes opened to the soft morning light splashed across the ceiling, dust motes drifting like slow-motion confetti. The storm inside her chest — the one that had lived there for years — was gone.

She smiled.

A real smile.

Jax stirred behind her, shifting closer, his voice low and rough from sleep.

"You're smiling."

"Am I?" she murmured.

"Yeah. I could feel it."

He pressed a small kiss into her shoulder — barely there, more like a thought than a touch — and she shivered.

"Good morning," he murmured.

She rolled gently to face him, their legs tangling without ceremony. His hair was a mess. His eyes half-lidded. The kind of soft, undone version of him she'd never gotten to see before.

"Hi," she whispered, brushing her nose lightly against his.

He smiled — slow, warm, so intimate it felt like another kind of kiss.

"You okay?" he asked softly.

"I'm better than okay," she said. "You?"

"Yeah." He tucked a strand of hair behind her ear. "Didn't think I'd sleep. But... with you..."

He shook his head once, as if trying to understand it himself. "It's the first full night I've had in months."

"Me too."

His thumb traced her cheekbone.

Her fingertips slid across his jaw.

Neither rushed.

Neither pulled away.

They just looked — really looked — like two people relearning the details they'd missed.

"Callie," he said quietly, "last night—"

She placed two fingers over his mouth.

"Jax. It wasn't a mistake."

He closed his eyes briefly, relief moving through him.

"Good," he whispered against her hand. "Because I'm not going anywhere."

She felt it — not as a promise but as truth.

Her truth.

His truth.

Their truth.

She leaned in and kissed him — slow, soft, morning-warm — the kind of kiss that wasn't about heat, or urgency, or declarations.

It was about simple, quiet happiness.

The first morning of something new.

His hand slid to her hip, steady and gentle.

Her fingers curled into the fabric of his shirt, pulling him closer until their foreheads touched.

"We should get up," she said eventually.

"We could," he murmured, lips brushing hers. "Or we could not."

She laughed — a sleepy, delighted sound that filled the room.

"Coffee?" she suggested.

"Hmm," he said, pretending to think. "You... or coffee..."

She raised an eyebrow. "Jax Hart. Are you choosing between me and caffeine?"

He ran a hand down her back, slow enough to make her breath catch. "You won."

"Well," she grinned, "that's something."

They got up together, reluctantly detangling, exchanging soft touches and half-kisses on the way to the kitchen. The early sun poured through the window, lighting up the dust on the benchtop, warming the timber floors.

Callie put on the kettle.

Jax leaned against the counter, watching her the way he used to — like he was memorising the moment.

"You know," she said, filling the kettle, "you're going to have to get used to this."

"Used to what?"

"Waking up next to me."

He pushed off the counter, moved behind her, slid his arms around her waist and kissed the back of her neck.

"That's the easiest adjustment I'll ever make."

She melted a little, leaning back into him.

The kettle clicked.

He didn't let her go.

She didn't want him to.

After a long, soft moment, he murmured against her skin, "What do you want today to look like?"

She smiled, turning in his arms. "Normal. With you in it."

He cupped her face, kissing her forehead, then her cheeks, then her mouth. "Done."

They sat at her tiny kitchen table, legs tangled under the chairs, mugs steaming between them. He reached for her hand without thinking. She let him have it without hesitation.

Outside, Crimson Creek woke slowly — footsteps on the pavement, a car passing, the river whispering under the bridge.

Inside, everything felt new.

Gentle.

Light.

Right.

"We can take this slow," he said softly. "Your pace. No pressure."

She squeezed his hand. "Jax... last night wasn't pressure. It was choice."

He nodded, eyes warm. "Then we choose again."

"We do," she said, kissing him softly.

When she pulled back, she whispered the words she'd been waiting years to say:

"Welcome home."

He breathed out, the faintest smile on his lips.

"I am."

36

CHAPTER 36: THE SHAPE OF AFTER

Crimson Creek, Queensland — The Mill, Next Day

By morning, the storm of sirens had thinned to paperwork and silence.

The Pegasus Mill felt smaller in daylight, like someone had turned the volume down on the shadows. Screens glowed with paused footage; evidence bags lay lined on the bench in neat rows. The word MINE stared up at them from inside one of the sleeves, the ink dried to a dull, harmless red.

Callie sat on the metal stool by the workbench, hands cupped around a mug she hadn't drunk from in ten minutes. The butterfly tape on her cheek had peeled a little at the corner. She didn't touch it. Some part of her liked the reminder – not of him, but of the fact she'd come through.

Across from her, Jax watched the door while pretending to read a report. His bandaged forearm rested on the table, the gauze stained a faint pink beneath fresh tape. His dog tags lay looped at his wrist, threaded through with a thin strip of crimson ribbon she recognised from her own gift jars.

Logan and Maya stood by the whiteboard, arguing quietly over arrows on the timeline.

"He escalated because he thought he was losing the narrative," Maya said, marker tapping the board. "Abduction, brick, the café performance – all about controlling the story."

"And then she rewrote his final scene," Logan replied. "Public. Loud.

Which, for the record, I'm framing on the wall of my mind."

Chase sat cross-legged on the floor, laptop balanced on his knees, fingers flying. A dozen stills tiled his screen: Noah at the door; the lens in the planter box; the carved words at the rail yard; the box on the counter, ribbon coiled like a threat that had finally snapped.

"I've mirrored the whole file tree," he said, not looking up. "Video, audio, text. If he so much as tries to claim this was 'misinterpreted affection' in front of a judge, we've got the receipts."

"Plural," Logan added. "In stereo."

Silence settled for a moment, heavy but not suffocating. The Mill hummed—generator, fans, the low, familiar vibration that had become the soundtrack of surviving.

Footsteps sounded on the stairs. Senior Constable Crowe appeared in the doorway, uniform neatly pressed, expression less sceptical than it had been a week ago.

"Morning," she said. "You lot look like death reheated."

"Flattered," Logan said. "What brings law enforcement to our humble den of iniquity?"

Crowe held up a folder. "Briggs was refused bail. His brief tried to play the 'helpful neighbour' card. Judge didn't buy it." Her gaze flicked to Callie. "He'll be held in remand till hearing. You won't see him on the street."

The words landed like small weights on a scale that had been tilted too long the wrong way. Callie's shoulders dropped a fraction.

"Thank you," she said.

Crowe cleared her throat, uncomfortable. "Your statement was solid. And the surveillance... well. Hard to argue with your own face on camera doing the wrong thing." She hesitated, then added, quieter, "For what it's worth, I'm sorry I didn't lean in sooner. Should've listened harder."

Callie blinked. Of all the things she'd braced for, that hadn't been one of them.

"You're listening now," she said. "That's going to matter for the next woman."

Something in Crowe's posture eased. "If you notice any copycats – well,

I'd say call us first, but I know how this lot operate." She tipped her chin at Jax and the others. "Just... don't forget we're here too."

"Duly noted," Logan said. "We'll try not to show you up too badly."

Crowe snorted, signed a form on Maya's clipboard, and left as briskly as she'd arrived. The echo of the door closing felt different this time. Less like dismissal. More like a line finally drawn on the right side of the law.

Chase whistled softly. "Did she just... apologise?"

"Mark the date," Maya said. "Someone bring me a calendar and a highlighter."

Callie smiled, faint but real. "Feels like the town's finally seeing the same picture we've been looking at."

"Because you held it up," Jax said.

She looked at him over the rim of the mug. "Pretty sure you lot had something to do with it."

"True," Logan said. "We make an excellent supporting cast."

He clapped his hands once, sharp. "All right, people. Victim no longer in immediate peril. Predator in a box. Time to talk aftercare."

Maya raised an eyebrow. "Is this the part where you recommend yoga and a podcast?"

"I was thinking more practical," he said. "The café window's still boarded. The chalkboard's out of date. The town's gossip quota is dangerously low. We need to give them a new story to tell."

Callie's fingers tightened around her mug. "A reopening?"

"A reclaiming," Maya corrected. "On your terms. When you're ready."

The thought made Callie's chest ache—not with dread this time, but with something that looked suspiciously like hope.

"Not tomorrow," she said. "But... soon. I want them to walk in and remember cinnamon and second-hand books, not the day the police dragged someone out in cuffs."

Logan shrugged. "We can help with that. I make a mean playlist and Chase can rig fairy lights like nobody's business."

Chase didn't look up from his code. "My lights have crushed men stronger than him."

Jax watched her quietly. "You tell us the date. We'll make sure the only thing that crosses that threshold is people who belong."

She met his gaze and saw it there, steady as ever—that mix of protectiveness and something softer he was still learning to name in daylight.

"Okay," she said, feeling the decision settle into place like a key turning. "Two weeks. Give the town time to stop buzzing and start missing their coffee."

Logan grinned. "Text that to the group chat or I'll forget and organise a parade by accident."

"We're not doing a parade," Maya said.

"Not with that attitude," he replied.

Callie's laugh came easier this time. "If there's a parade, I'm moving."

Jax's mouth tipped. "I'll help you pack."

The banter circled, gentle, cushioning. Underneath it, something in Callie's bones exhaled. The danger wasn't gone—danger never really left— but the sharp edges had dulled. The story had turned its page.

Crimson Creek — Late Afternoon

They walked back to the café in the kind of light that made Crimson Creek look almost pretty. The storm had scrubbed the sky clean; the river moved slow and brown under the bridge, carrying yesterday away in small, unremarkable ripples.

Red Wolf Books & Brew stood with its boarded window and faded chalkboard, looking both wounded and stubborn. Someone—Mrs Keegan, if Callie had to guess—had tucked a small bunch of flowers into the wire of the security grate. The petals were already starting to brown in the sun.

"Looks like you've got fans," Logan said.

"Or a secret admirer with very low-budget taste," Chase added.

"Behave," Maya said, swatting his arm.

Callie reached out and adjusted the little bundle, fingers gentle. "It's enough."

Inside, the café smelled like dust and the ghost of coffee. The air held a faint metallic tang from where the broken glass had been swept away. The boarded pane threw the light off, making the room feel narrower, but the bones were the same—tables, shelves, the coffee machine sitting on the counter like it had been waiting.

Jax closed the door behind them and flipped the lock. The soft click felt like drawing a breath.

"All right," Logan said. "Operation Resurrection. Where do we start?"

"Window," Callie said. "Feels like a room can't breathe properly if it can't see out."

"Already on the books," Maya replied. "Legit glazier, vetted, background check clear. They're booked for Monday."

Callie raised an eyebrow. "You did a background check on a window guy?"

Maya didn't look apologetic. "We're thorough. Also, he makes scones. His Google reviews are near-religious."

Logan rolled his shoulders. "I'll scrub the outside walls, fix the chalkboard, and charm the neighbours into dropping by on opening day."

"Charming, yes," Maya said dryly. "Subtle, no."

Chase lifted the trapdoor behind the counter, disappearing down the short flight of steps to the store room. "I'll check the wiring and re-run the security feed. And install a new panic button that actually works when someone leans on it, not just when they're rearranging muffins."

"And you?" Callie asked Jax.

His answer was simple. "Whatever you need."

She looked around, taking stock—not of damage, but of what would stay. The mug rack her mum had loved. The second-hand fiction shelf. The little chalk fox someone's kid had drawn on the back wall and she'd never had the heart to erase.

"Paint," she said finally. "That back corner. It still smells like him. I want it to smell like fresh."

He nodded. "Done."

They worked for hours, the café slowly shrugging off its haunted air. Logan dragged the tables out, scrubbed the floor with a ferocity that bordered on spiritual cleansing, and complained loud enough to keep the mood from sinking.

"Who knew coffee could bond with tiles like this?" he groaned, attacking a stubborn stain.

"It's not the coffee," Callie said, wiping down the bookshelves. "It's the sugar."

"Metaphor," Maya said from the doorway, where she was talking to the glazier on the phone. "Sweetness will always leave a mark."

"Put that on a T-shirt," Chase called from under the counter. "I'll buy two."

By the time the light shifted toward late afternoon, the place looked less like a crime scene and more like a café mid-renovation. The board remained over the window for now, but someone had drawn a little wolf head in the corner in white marker. Callie suspected Logan.

She stood in the middle of the room, hand on her hip, breathing in the new mix of scents—cleaner, dust, the faint citrus of the oil she'd wiped the tables with.

"It's strange," she said softly. "It's the same space. But it feels... different."

"Because the story's yours again," Jax said.

She turned to look at him. He had a line of white paint across one forearm where he'd leaned against the wall; his shirt clung damp at the throat. For the first time in days, the lines around his eyes looked less cut in.

"Do you ever get tired?" she asked. "Of always being on guard?"

"Sometimes," he admitted. "But then a day like today happens and I remember why I started. There's something satisfying about putting the world back where it should be, even if it's just one room at a time."

She stepped closer, the sounds of Logan and Chase bickering in the storeroom fading to a distant hum.

"And what about you?" she asked quietly. "Where do you go when this is over? Another town? Another mess?"

He hesitated. For a man who could make tactical decisions in half a heartbeat, the question seemed to take him longer.

"Pegasus offered to keep a permanent post here," he said. "Regional anchor. Fewer flights. More ground work. More..." He gestured vaguely at the café. "Community."

"More coffee," she supplied.

"That too."

"Is that what you want?" she asked. Not what he thought he owed. Not what duty demanded. Just that.

He met her eyes, steady and unhurried. "I want to wake up in a place where I know what the river sounds like. Where I can sit in that corner—" he nodded at the table by the window "—and pretend I'm just a guy answering emails while the woman he loves makes coffee behind the counter."

The word sat there between them, unflinching.

"Loves," she repeated, tasting it.

He didn't look away. "Yeah."

Her breath hitched. Not because it surprised her, but because hearing it in daylight felt like putting something fragile out where wind could find it.

"You're allowed to want that," she said.

"So are you."

She thought of her mother's hospice window, the night before he'd left. The anger, the grief, the hollow where his absence had lived. She thought of the Mill, the cabin, the way his hand had found hers in the dark without hesitating.

"I used to believe I only got to choose between being safe and being loved," she said. "That if I let someone close, I'd just be handing them better tools to hurt me with."

"And now?" he asked.

She looked around the café—the boards on the window, the cleaned tables, the new paint. The Pegasus team in the background, loud and imperfect and entirely hers in ways that had nothing to do with blood.

"Now I think maybe being loved is part of being safe," she said. "If it's the right person."

He swallowed, the movement visible in his throat. "Am I the right person?"

She stepped closer until their bodies shared the same small patch of air.

"You were always the right person," she said. "We just had terrible timing."

A slow, helpless smile tugged at his mouth. "We can fix timing."

She slid her fingers down his paint-marked forearm, feeling the warmth of his skin beneath the thin layer. "Yeah," she said. "I think we can."

He dipped his head to kiss her, gentle and sure. This wasn't the desperate clutch of people wondering if they'd make it through the night. This was two people who had, and were choosing each other with their eyes open.

When they drew apart, Logan's voice floated out from the storeroom.

"For the record," he called, "if you're going to snog in the workplace, at least let me turn the cameras off. Chase is going to have a field day scrubbing the feeds."

"Already marked that segment for deletion," Chase said. "I'm not emotionally equipped to watch my own boss make heart eyes."

Maya strolled in, hands in her pockets, expression smug. "He's lying. He's absolutely saving a copy for the training file labelled 'What Boundaries Look Like.'"

Callie laughed, cheeks warm, and didn't move away from Jax.

"This is harassment," Jax said mildly.

"This is team bonding," Logan corrected. "Also, Cal, before I forget—half the town's asked when you're opening. Mrs Keegan, the postie, the high school science teacher, three teenagers who think your hot chocolate is a religious experience, and a very confused tourist who thought this was a laundromat."

"A laundromat?" Callie echoed.

"Don't ask," Maya said. "We live in strange times."

Callie shook her head, smiling. "Two weeks," she repeated. "We'll do a soft opening first. Friends, regulars. Keep it low-key."

Logan frowned theatrically. "You are killing me with this 'low-key' obsession."

"You'll cope," she said. "You can make a playlist."

His sour look dissolved. "Fine. But I'm sneaking one power ballad in. For emotional closure."

"Choose wisely," Maya warned. "I have veto power."

Callie listened to them spar and felt the knot in her chest loosen another notch. This—this mess of sarcasm and planning and paint under fingernails—this was the shape of after.

Crimson Creek — Later That Night

The others drifted out as the sky darkened. Logan headed back to the Switchyard to terrorise the beer taps. Maya went to her rented unit with three case files and a promise to "sleep at some point." Chase stayed long enough to finish securing the new camera mounts, then vanished into the Mill with a yawn and a half-wave.

Callie and Jax lingered in the café after the last engine noise had faded. The room felt oddly large without the others, their voices still echoing faintly off the high ceilings.

She perched on a stool at the counter, legs swinging, watching him flip the chairs onto the tables.

"You know," she said, "you're very domestic for someone who knows six ways to kill a man with a spoon."

"Seven," he said. "And I make a mean omelette."

"I'm unexpectedly comforted."

He set the last chair down and turned to her, wiping his hands on a cloth. "You okay staying at the flat tonight? We can do another Mill sleepover if you'd rather."

She thought of the apartment—the boarded lounge window already measured for replacement, the familiar creak in the hallway floor, her mum's photo on the kitchen shelf.

"I want to go home," she said. "I don't mean the Mill or the cabin. I mean my actual home. My bed. My chipped mug. The light that comes through the curtains at exactly six-oh-seven every morning."

He nodded. "Then that's what we do. I'll crash on the couch until the window's fixed."

She raised an eyebrow. "You? On my couch? You're six foot and my sofa's offended by tall people."

He shrugged. "I've slept in worse places. Besides, consider it a field test. If it complains, we'll guilt it into cooperation."

She hopped down from the stool and came around the counter to him. The café felt smaller suddenly—not in a bad way, but in the way a room shrinks when it's only got two people left and everything important is between them.

"Jax," she said. "When the café's open again and the town goes back to worrying about rates and parking and the price of milk... what do we look like?"

"Humans," he said. "Possibly undercaffeinated ones."

She swatted his arm. "I'm serious."

"So am I."

He took a breath, expression softening. "I see you at the machine, lecturing someone on the art of a proper flat white. I see me at that table, pretending to work while I actually watch you because I haven't got tired of the miracle of you existing in the same room yet."

She smiled, eyes shining a little. "And at night?"

"At night," he said slowly, "I see us fighting over who gets the good pillow and whose turn it is to pretend they like my cooking."

"You really are bad at romance speeches," she said, even as her chest went warm.

"I could say the words, Callie. The big ones. But they're only worth anything if I back them with a thousand small, boring, ordinary days." He lifted a shoulder. "I want those with you. The boring ones. The mornings where nothing happens except you burn the toast and I swear I can fix the toaster."

"I don't burn toast," she objected automatically.

"You will when you're distracted."

"By what?"

He leaned in, very slightly. "Me."

Her heart gave an unhelpful, delighted lurch.

"That was almost smooth," she said.

"I'm practising," he murmured.

She looked up at him, really looked, at the man who had once left and come back harder, quieter, but still the boy who had sat with her in hospital corridors and drunk terrible vending machine coffee just to have something to do with his hands.

"I want that too," she said. "The ordinary. The messy. The mornings where you track mud into the kitchen and I pretend not to care."

"You'll care," he said.

"I'll care," she agreed. "And I'll still choose you."

The air between them shifted, soft and certain. He reached out, brushed a loose strand of hair behind her ear, fingers lingering.

"Okay then," he said quietly. "Here's my official, on-record statement: I'm not going anywhere. Crimson Creek is my post for as long as they'll have me. You are—"

She put a hand on his chest, stopping him, not because she didn't want to hear it, but because some things she wanted to meet halfway.

"I know," she said. "Me too."

He smiled, that small, unguarded one that still surprised her. "I'm still going to say it," he warned.

"Later," she said. "When we're not standing in the middle of my workplace and Logan isn't lurking in some camera feed hoping for content."

He laughed, a low, warm sound. "Fair point."

She slipped her hand down his arm and laced their fingers. "Come on. Take me home."

He locked up behind them, the café lights winking out one by one. The street was quiet—just the murmur of distant traffic and the river's slow whisper. As they walked, his hand stayed in hers, easy and unhurried.

For the first time in a long time, Callie didn't glance over her shoulder.

She looked forward.

✦ ✦ ✦

Crimson Creek — A Few Days Later

The paint dried. The new glass went in, bright and clear, smelling faintly of solvent and start-over. The glazier, who did indeed make scones worth a minor religious movement, refused payment for the labour on the grounds that "the town owes you at least a window."

Mara Bell dropped by once, recorder tucked away, just to deliver a simple line: "When you're ready to tell it, it's your story, not his," and left a card with a small wolf doodled on it.

The teenagers who worshipped her hot chocolate taped a hand-drawn sign to the door: WE'RE WAITING, RED WOLF. NO PRESSURE, BUT WE'RE DYING.

Mrs Keegan brought over a pot plant and set it on the windowsill with a pat of the soil, announcing, "Every café needs something green that isn't envy."

Each gesture stitched the wound a little smaller.

In the evenings, when the Mill hummed with other cases and the café lights were dark, Callie and Jax sat on her couch—too short for him, as predicted—sharing takeaway and stupid TV shows. Sometimes they talked about the heavy things. Sometimes they didn't.

She woke from nightmares less and less. When she did, his hand was there, steady, no questions asked unless she wanted them.

On the night she chose the date for the reopening, she wrote it on the chalkboard herself.

TWO WEEKS.

Her hand shook once. Then steadied.

"You sure?" Jax asked, leaning in the doorway.

She looked at the words, at the small crimson wolf she drew next to them. "Yeah," she said. "I'm done letting fear pick my calendar."

He came up behind her, wrapped his arms around her waist, and rested his chin on her shoulder. In the reflection of the window, she could see them—the café, the town beyond, the two of them framed in a world that was still cracked in places but undeniably theirs.

"When they come through that door," he said, "what do you want them to see first?"

"Coffee," she joked, then sobered. "Me. Whole. Not just as the woman something bad happened to."

"They'll see it," he said. "Because it's true."

She reached up and traced his dog tags where they lay at his wrist, tied with the strip of crimson.

"And you?" she asked. "What do you want them to see when they look at you?"

"Security," he said. "And a guy who's very clearly, very stupidly in love with the owner."

She smiled, the kind of smile that came from somewhere deeper than her mouth. "Good. That's exactly what they're getting."

She stood there a long time after he'd gone to lock the back door, looking at the chalk letters and the tiny wolf, at the reflections of the shelves and tables and empty chairs.

Tomorrow, she thought, would be about coffee and conversation and the relentless normalcy of everyday life.

The day after that would be, too.

And in two weeks' time, she'd stand in the doorway with scissors in her hand, the crimson ribbon fluttering against the cream paint, and the whole town watching.

She wasn't afraid of that anymore.

She was ready.

37

EPILOGUE — ALWAYS YOURS

Crimson Creek — Two Weeks Later

The ribbon fluttered in the afternoon breeze, crimson against the soft cream of the café doorway. Jax had tied it himself that morning—steady hands, focused expression, a faint smile he didn't bother hiding when he looked at her.

The sign above gleamed new:

RED WOLF BOOKS & BREW.

Fresh charcoal paint. Clean, sharp lettering. A wolf silhouette etched beside the name like a promise.

The broken windows were gone.

The splintered door replaced.

The varnish still held the faint sweetness of new beginnings beneath the scent of roasted beans and cinnamon.

Callie stood at the threshold, scissors in hand.

Her palm trembled—not with fear, but with the strange lightness that comes when something heavy finally, finally lets go. Behind her, the café hummed with warmth: the quiet clatter of Logan adjusting the playlist, Maya wiping a fingerprint off the counter like it was a national security breach, and Chase pretending not to hover near the espresso machine with God-knows-what update queued on his tablet.

Outside, the footpath was full.

People she knew.

People she'd only seen in passing.

People who'd whispered her name in worry weeks ago and now stood here with cautious smiles, warm eyes, and paper cones of flowers tucked into elbows.

Mrs Keegan waved a flag she had absolutely made at home.

The teenagers who worshipped her hot chocolate wore "WE SURVIVED WITHOUT YOU" shirts.

Even Senior Constable Crowe was there, arms folded, expression almost soft.

Maya leaned against the lamppost, sunglasses hiding a smirk.

Chase tried to look like he wasn't recording.

Logan absolutely was.

And Jax—

Jax stood just behind her, close enough that she could feel the warmth of him at her back, not touching, just there. Steady. Grounded. Present.

He murmured, low and warm, "You ready?"

She exhaled.

Smile soft.

Heart full.

"Yeah," she said. "I really am."

Logan cupped his hands around his mouth. "All right, Red Wolf! Let's see the legendary ceremonial snip before the crowd mutinies. Some of us need caffeine to live!"

Laughter rippled through the street.

Callie lifted the scissors.

Jax leaned in, his voice a soft thread meant only for her.

"No matter what comes next... I'm here. You don't do any of this alone again."

She swallowed once, hard—but the good kind.

The kind that meant emotion, not fear.

"I know," she whispered.

She cut the ribbon.

The crowd erupted—cheers, applause, someone whistling like they'd won a prize. Logan pumped a fist. Chase lifted his tablet high. Mrs Keegan dabbed her eyes with a tissue embroidered with daisies.

Callie stepped inside first, the bell above the door chiming bright and clear.

It didn't sound like the chime of an ending.

It sounded like a beginning.

Customers streamed in—carefully, excitedly, reverently. The café filled with the soft chaos of life returning: chairs scraping, mugs clinking, familiar greetings bouncing off the restored glass.

Jax watched her greet the first customer with a warm smile, watched her move behind the counter like she'd never left, watched her reclaim every inch of her space.

He didn't hover.

He didn't scan the room like a threat lurked behind the pastries.

He simply took his seat at the table by the window—his table—and let the morning wrap around him like sunlight.

He looked different like this.

Not the soldier on alert.

Not the agent in the shadows.

Just the man who'd found the place he wanted to stay.

Callie made two flat whites—hers and his—and set one down in front of him with a quiet, knowing smile.

"Welcome to Red Wolf," she teased softly.

He reached for her fingers, brushing them with his thumb. "Always."

Her heart kicked, warm and certain.

"Don't get comfortable. The toaster's still moody."

"I'll negotiate," he said. "I speak fluent appliance."

She rolled her eyes. "You speak fluent trouble."

"Yours," he corrected gently.

Her breath caught.

He didn't look away.

"Always yours."

Callie blinked against the sudden sting in her eyes—this time, the good kind, the kind that meant healing had reached all the way in.

Outside, the afternoon shimmered.

Inside, the café hummed.

And for the first time in longer than she could measure, Callie Hart—owner, survivor, lover, no longer afraid—felt the world settle exactly where it was supposed to be.

Beside him.

With him.

For whatever came next.

Because they had walked through hell, and somehow, impossibly, beautifully, found their way back to each other.

Always yours.

And always—

home.

A Sneak Peek at....

Book Two — Reckless Sins
A Pegasus Special Security Novel
by Stephanie Colson

Crimson Creek — Four Months Later
Nightfall

The first bullet wasn't meant for Maya Quinn.

The second was.

She knew that the moment the alley exploded with echo and heat — muzzle flash ripping through the dark like the city had torn open its own throat. Her boots skidded on wet concrete as she dove behind a dumpster, breath burning her lungs.

"Quinn, move!" Logan's voice crackled in her comm, tight with panic she'd never heard from him. "Sniper. Rooftop. Two o'clock!"

"I know!" she hissed, pressing her spine into cold metal, counting heartbeats she didn't have time for.

Another shot screamed past, close enough to kiss the loose strand of hair at her temple.

Okay.

So someone wanted her dead.

Again.

But this time felt different — cleaner, colder.

Personal.

Maya wiped blood from her cheek where shrapnel had kissed her. "This was supposed to be a simple intel meet."

"Yeah, well," Logan growled, "since when do you do simple?"

A shadow moved on the rooftop. Tall. Fluid. Precise.

Whoever he was, he wasn't guessing.

He was hunting.

"Logan," she said, low and controlled. "I need eyes."

"I'm three blocks out—"

"I need them *now*."

Silence. A curse. Then the sound of Logan sprinting, breath ragged but determined.

"Quinn, stay down," he ordered. "If you die before I get there, I'm bringing you back to punch you."

Her lips twitched — the smallest almost-smile in a death-tight moment.

Then the sniper fired again.

Brick shattered inches from her head. Dust rained down.

Maya rolled, fast, using the blast of noise as cover. Her gun came up. Her breath stilled.

And then she saw him.

The rooftop figure stepped into the glow of a distant streetlamp just long enough for her to catch the shape of his jaw, the cut of his shoulders, and the unmistakable glint of a tattoo along his forearm — a pattern she knew like old scars.

Her blood froze.

No.

No.

This was impossible.

But the target moved with the exact rhythm of a ghost she'd buried.

A ghost they'd all buried.

"Maya," Logan panted through comms. "Talk to me. What do you see?"

Her hand shook.

"Nothing," she lied.

Because if she said his name aloud

— *if she admitted he was alive* —

the world she'd rebuilt would crumble.

Including the part of it where Logan's heart touched hers.

The shooter raised his rifle.

Maya whispered to the dark, "Not tonight."

She fired once — clean, sharp, controlled.

The rooftop figure slipped back into shadow.

Gone.

Bootsteps pounded at the alley mouth. Logan rounded the corner, breath harsh, eyes wild.

"Maya!" He grabbed her shoulders, checking for wounds. "Did he hit you?"

She shook her head once.

"Talk to me," he demanded, voice fierce and afraid. "Who the hell was on that roof?"

Her throat worked.

She almost said his name.

Almost broke the world.

Instead, she whispered the only truth she could give him:

"It wasn't a stranger."

Logan's eyes darkened.

Everything changed in that heartbeat.

And far above the alley, unseen, a man with a familiar tattoo watched them both with a smile that did not reach his eyes.

Reckless Sins

Coming Soon in the Pegasus Special Security Series
Dark secrets.
Old loves.

A ghost they should have let stay dead.
And a betrayal that will break more than hearts.

✦ ✦ ✦

About the Author

Stephanie Colson is an Australian romantic-suspense author known for her fierce heroines, emotionally charged plots, and the electrifying chemistry that runs through every page of her Pegasus Special Security and Blaire Hunter series. Her stories blend danger, passion, and deeply human characters who fight for love even when the world turns against them.

When she's not writing twist-filled thrillers with heat and heart, Stephanie can be found reading by the ocean, exploring cafés across NSW, or dreaming up the next couple who won't let her sleep until their story is told. She believes in strong coffee, slow burns, and love worth surviving for.

Stephanie writes full-time from Australia, where she lives with far too many notebooks and a growing stack of draft manuscripts.

You can connect with me on:
f https://www.facebook.com/profile.php?id=61585228183518

Also by Stephanie Colson

Stephanie Colson writes romantic suspense filled with danger, loyalty, and impossible choices — stories where love is tested under fire and survival is never guaranteed.

Book 2 – Reckless Sins

Logan Kane has lived by one rule—never touch his best friend's little sister.

Emma's the temptation he's resisted since high school: brilliant, stubborn, far too good for the ex-soldier with blood on his hands.

When she inherits a bar caught in a rival's crossfire, Logan's forced to step in as her shield. But one reckless kiss shatters every promise, and the line between loyalty and desire disappears.

Protecting her means betraying a brother. Loving her might save him anyway.

Book 3 – Ruthless Vows

To keep her inheritance—and her life—Lily needs a husband on paper.

Enter Nate Cross: combat veteran, security specialist, and the only man she's ever truly feared wanting.

A fake marriage was supposed to be simple business. But living under one roof with a man who sees through every lie is anything but safe.

As her stalker closes in, vows forged in deception ignite into something fierce and real... and neither of them may survive the truth.